¡PÓNK!

CLAYTON

INK!

NIGHTBOAT BOOKS

NEW YORK

Copyright © 2025 by Marcus Clayton

All rights reserved
Printed in the United States

ISBN: 978-1-643-62243-9

Design and typesetting by Kit Schluter
Typeset in Sabon and RixStamp_Pro

Cataloging-in-publication data is available
from the Library of Congress

Nightboat Books
New York
www.nightboat.org

For Marlén

Tracklisting

Everything will be permitted in the dance circle... for in fact the sole purpose of the gathering is to let the supercharged libido and the stifled aggressiveness spew out volcanically. Symbolic killings, figurative cavalcades, and imagined multiple murders, everything has to come out. The ill humors seep out, tumultuous as lava flows.

FRANTZ FANON

It's silly, no?
When a rocket ship explodes
and everybody still wants to fly.

PRINCE

Nothing is more punk rock than surviving in a hungry sea of white noise.

HANIF ABDURRAQIB

The Ally

The ally is a punk rocker.

The ally knows the dance. The mosh pit—a word birthed from a Black mouth no matter what white boys tell you. The thesis of this dance: keep bodies safe, move as they move.

Say nothing.

Listen.

Noise coats the punks in a blanket to warm their bones. They huddle like sticks to become fire that illuminates, not burns. In that light, under the blanket, they see themselves in the dance: the Black boys, the brown boys, the girls, the femmes, the Natives, the Asians, the trans, the bi, the gays, the lesbians, the impaired, the poor, the bodies freezing on the margins whose identity does not have enough shelter. They all move to the rhythms painted in the same blues.

They all sing punk songs of the ancestors.

The punks sing Los Saicos.

The punks sing Death's "Politicians in My Eyes."

The punks sing Pure Hell, who reconstructed white lyrics,

> *Well, these boots are made for walking*
> *And that's just what they'll do*
> *One of these days these boots*
> *Are gonna walk all over you.*

Learn. The mosh pit is a pogo. Collective imbalances where bodies trust each other to catch the other. To shove someone in the pit should be a defensive motion to assuage collision, to exhaust pressure from the bones, to make sure none of them break. These

3

crashes are inevitable, stability impossible. If someone falls, stop. Pick them up. Don't let their skull powder under Doc Martens and Chucks. If someone wants to crowd surf, and they ask permission, and the timing is there, lift them above your head.

Let them fly.

But know, sometimes, the ally fails. Example. Straight hands in a queer pit. The ally watches his hands when a femme crowd-surfs because safety is priority. The lower back, shoulders, calves, neck, stomach, and shins are all fine places to hold someone's balance above.

If the ally thinks about his own dick while trying to catch breasts, ass, mouths, or crotch for too long, the music will stop. ~~The ally~~ will no longer be the ally. ~~The ally~~ will be punished with the same erasure they forced onto othered lives. The ally's name will be struck from the genre's archives, a reminder of truths they refused to believe. Then ~~the ally~~ will be swiftly exiled from punk.

\\   //

Listen.

White punks scream. Their swastikas chase away the pogo, use boots to goose-step Black and brown punks out of clubs meant to be sanctuaries.

White punk is not a mosh pit.

White punk is a slam dance.

Watch them steal Caribbean moves,
turn Jamaican rude boys into bastards.

Elbows aim for jaws.

Fists are waves crashing like cop slugs mutilating unarmed faces.

White punk is poison.

Watch.

They stomp on the roots to extinguish punks on the margin.

We say,
Be punk like Marvin Gaye is punk.
Like Prince is punk.

> White punk says,
> Marvin Gaye and Prince are not punk.
> That's soul and shit.

We say,
Soul is punk.

> White punk says,
> Where's the guitar?
> Punk needs guitar.

We say,
Punk does not need guitar.
Prince has a guitar,
But he don't need no guitar
to be punk.

> White punk says,
> Nah, man. Punk is loud.

We say,
It *is* loud.

> White punk says,
> Punk is angry.

We say,
It *is* angry.

> White punk says,
> Punk hates the man.

We say,
Punk *does* hate the man.

                                        White punk says,
                                    Punk does not conform.

We say,
No, sir.

                                        White punk says,
                                         Punk is . . .

We say,
Black.

                                        White punk says,
                                       Punk is FEAR.

We say,
Lee Ving calls a 1981 crowd "a bunch of fags"
then gets into a fistfight with a woman on stage.

                                        White punk says,
                                    Punk is Minor Threat.

We say,
Ian MacKaye writes "Guilty of Being White,"
equates white fragility to Black oppression.
Any other opinion is erasure of his experience
as a white man in Black neighborhoods.

                                        White punk says,
                                   Punk is the Sex Pistols.

We say,
Never Mind the Bollocks, Here's the Sex Pistols
replaces Blackness with fashion,
and let's be honest: they're a fucking boy band.

The punks sing The Bags, *We don't need the English telling us
what should be.*

The punks sing Marvin, *Make me wanna holler the way they
do my life—
Make me wanna holler and throw up both my hands.*

The punks sing Linda Lindas, *Poser! Blockhead! Riffraff! Jerkface!*

Learn.

                    Listen.

          Punk can be a teacher.
          Offer dance steps to survive whiteness,
          survive Nazi elbows that want to break jaws in the mosh pit.
          Can teach community to exist without violence
          should they choose
          at least without the tools.
          When the punk sings Audre, *The master's tools will never
          dismantle the master's house. They may allow us
          to temporarily beat him at his own game, but they will never
          enable us to bring about genuine change.*
          Or maybe the punk wants to sing Claudia's *Citizen*, all of it.
          The amalgam voice a chorus making hardships tangible
          that white folk think are pure fiction. Words—
          fiction, nonfiction, *based* on nonfiction.
          The ally knows, within the bones, the words are true.

Punk wants to sing the good notes
the rhythm *and* the blues
to make the harmonies glimmer
in the tenderness of punk rock voices.

The punks sing Malcolm, *The fox acts friendly toward the lamb,
and usually the fox is the one who ends up with lambchop on his
plate.*

\\   //

Watch Bikini Kill—riot grrrl queens, scream *girls to the front*
to keep the macho bullshit away from femme punk bodies in the
mosh pit; excrete feminism into the punk clubs when Nazi punks
and jocks threatened the scenes in the early '90s. Bikini Kill physically removed violent men at their shows when necessary. Once the
intruders were gone, they continued to play cramped clubs humid
with sweating bodies like their DIY ancestors.

They are the ally. They are rewarded decades later with reunion
shows. They play to a following so large, their shows end up sold
out in the 3,800-person capacity Hollywood Palladium. They are
the ally, so they bring punks of color with them.

The Linda Lindas open.

Alice Bag opens.

~~Fuck U Pay Us open.~~

~~Outside the venue, when Fuck U Pay Us leave the stage—an
all-Black, nonbinary femme, queer, reparations punk band—singer
Jasmine Nyende is not allowed back inside the venue, shoved away
from the entrance by security for not having the "correct" credentials.
Forced to piss on the cold concrete instead of their promised green
room. Promised they would be taken care of by their allies, now
being told *I'll take care of you, alright* by predatory security guards.~~

~~Then the misgendering of Uhuru Moor. The dead naming. Fuck~~

~~U Pay Us martyred in the name of the white punk scratching to be~~
~~called the ally. The rhythm. The dance.~~
~~Bikini Kill say nothing for days. At best, they post on social~~
~~media. Below a picture of Bikini Kill blissfully playing to a theater~~
~~full of feminist punks young and old, they write admonishing~~
~~security who should have done better. Bikini Kill hopes this never~~
~~happens again because they are the ally.~~

\\   //

Fuck their redactions.
Hear them loud: the rhythm and the blues.
Real punk motherfuckers.
All Black, all femme, on a grand Los Angeles stage.
In front of them are white faces who paid mountains of coin to
see punk rock.
That's ok.
They watch an all-Black, all-femme band of real punk mother-
fuckers.
For at least thirty minutes, the only punk rockers in the world.
Jasmine Nyende wears a wedding gown to a funeral in service
for their silence. Their face painted white, they croon over Uhuru
Moor's spaced-out guitar riffs like a child of Hendrix. Black femmes
consent their screams. Reparations within the reverberations—

> The punks sing Fuck U Pay Us, *People over property! People*
> *over property! People over property!*
> *We will watch the empire fall! We will watch the empire*
> *fall! We will watch*
> *the empire fall!*
> *We will*
> *watch*
> *the empire fall!*

They sing.
They sing.
They sing.

                              Real

              punk

                                            mother

                    fuckers

\\   //

              know the dance moves
              on the frontlines
              pick us up
              let us fly.
              Floating tender in the sky.
              Promise.
              We fly.

¡PÓNK!

In Three Acts

Act I

White punks don't give a shit about us. They're scowling statues, at best tolerating the space we take from them. We set up our equipment for a gig at a run-down pizza parlor in Bend, Oregon. Our first show outside of Southern California and our own punk circles. The scowls know who we are, though; our name seared into their local flyers—multicolored papers decomposing in gutters like the autumn leaves we stepped on to get inside the venue. We are Pipebomb! and we are more punk than all these white grimaces combined.

On drums, Id y Yacht, real name [Redacted]. Our token white, our ally, our beast. His blast beats create quakes to shatter dance floors and force feet to move. Look at his clothes: Richard Spencer haircut to trick white punks into false safety, checkered dress shirt and khakis straight from work, suede laced boots he bought from a yard sale at Exene Cervenka's home.

On bass and vox, [Redacted—his identity is his own to share, to keep, to want], better known to us as Upper Duck. He plays duct-taped instruments, wears a black Cannibal Corpse T-shirt, wears a Mexican mustache gifted by his father's genes, wears jet-black hair molded by Suavecito pomade. Duck knows little of his father's language, and his skin is glossed light like his ancestor's Spanish colonizers, but he screams *Chicano* while refusing American flags.

On guitar and other vox [I don't wear the name picked by Mamá and Pops. I wish I could tell them the name is not in a garbage bin, but a closet with a nice wooden hanger. For now], Blacky Moose. These days, Moose. Only Moose. I am covered in roses, designs stitched into a white short-sleeve button-up, tucked into torn black jeans covering filthy black and white Chucks. A beard shields my face, tattoos coat the high yellow of my right arm [I swear it is not a shame—both my parents never told one another that they wanted a child a shade browner, a shade Blacker. When I happened, all they could do was compromise], and dark brown dreadlocks cage my eyes from direct contact with punks [most effective months from now when Pipebomb! plays a show in Anaheim, CA, southeast of our hometowns in Southeast LA. Los Angeles punks know of us, or at least know the exclamation point is part of the aesthetic. Some know our punk names but remain unaware that I dropped "Blacky" before the Bend show.

"You're Blacky, right?" a drunk man asks at the Anaheim show.

"Just Moose," I say.

"Oh, ok," he relents. "Is that an Indian flag?"

Over my amplifier, I hang a Costa Rican flag. Being mixed, strangers make a game out of guessing my ethnicities. *You're Black and something else,* which is true. Sometimes people know my other half is Latino. Other times, I get something like, *Croatian, or Hawaiian, or half white*—the latter of which physically hurts me, so the flag helps me avoid the pain.

"It's the Costa Rican flag," I say, proud.

"Oh, you like Costa Rica?" a drunk man asks at the Anaheim show.

"I'm half Costa Rican."

"I see," he says. "You know, I've been to Belize."

"Tight."

After the show, we wheel our equipment past white punks who say things like, *They're not really punk. Songs about Black or brown power or whatever shit? Thinkin' they're MLK or some bullshit? Nah. They slow down too much, pretendin' to be Fugazi. Thinkin' too hard instead of just lettin' loose and breaking shit. Motherfucker was wearing flowers on his shirt, for Christ's sake. They ain't gritty like Agnostic Front or Minor Threat. You can't convince me that band knows anything about the streets.* My dreadlocks save me, stop me from placing a face to the words. I do not see all the punks huddled around curbsides and streetlights smoking cigarettes and using their phones. All of them white. Duck and I transform into splotches. I do not see Yacht's mouth when he screams "POSERS!" at the crowd who did not care for us. Duck and I always assume it's meant to protect his friends, but can never deny that it's an eternal amends for his white guilt. Duck and I tolerate Yacht's guilt. Sometimes it is quite nice, the backsplash of penance.

Yacht is a homeowner, son of one-percenters, full-time college instructor, has an affinity for white straight-edged hardcore. But his disdain for his whiteness makes him hate everything he owns. The nice cars, the clean clothes, the crisp dollar bills perpetually in his wallet, specifically to give to unhoused folks. In those moments, if Duck and I are around, I pretend I do not have cash while Duck yells something like, *I ain't givin' you meth money!*

Yacht especially hates his beautiful house. He and his wife live in the heart of Anaheim, inheriting his parent's five-bedroom, three-bathroom home, with the backyard and the garage with room for two cars plus storage. I try to be happy for him, but Yacht is very clear about how storing the treadmill in his childhood bedroom did not erase the traumas living as ghosts within the house's walls— things I can't repeat, things I have personally never endured, and things I tried to bury by changing the subject as swiftly as possible.

"So, which bathroom is the better bathroom?"

The downstairs one, apparently.

It never surprises me, then, when Yacht feels the need to intervene in whiteness when it confronts either Duck or me. Protecting us, even when we don't ask. At the Anaheim show, as I pack my equipment into the van, I do not see Yacht come face to face with a white punk bedazzled in metal studs and FEAR patches, bright red mohawk stretching into the sky like a war missile. I hear, *I just don't care about spic and nigger songs, bro*, and I hear the crash of bone on teeth and bedazzled studs colliding with the ground. The noise reverberates within the cavern of my hair. I do not see Duck pull Yacht away, and I do not hear him say, *Fuck these foos. We got better shows coming up, anyway.* I see nothing.

But right now,] about a hundred punks stand in the pizza parlor. This is the largest audience we've ever had. All the white punks wear the costumes: studded leather everything, multicolored mohawks, black shitkickers galore, stick and poke tattoos inked by jittery friends. Many of them coked out of their minds; a blonde girl wearing a GBH shirt twirls around in the pit before we play any songs, her pupils dilated enough for me to see. There are Black and brown punks in here, sure. They line the back of the parlor, wallflowers kicked out of the center by the violent typhoons of white slam dancers.

Every scowling face in front of us has skin the shade of chalk, and stands with arms crossed in defiance of our presence [this is the default back home in Los Angeles too. Even in our hometown, bookers often ask Pipebomb! to play a show at the last minute, preying on our desperation for booking, praying Duck and I stand in front to show diversity. These are the shows that tuck us away at 1 a.m. on a five-band bill—a packed house from 9 p.m. to 11:30 pm, but folks get tired after midnight, so we play to a promoter and a couple of unlucky friends.

I am being harsh. I apologize. Los Angeles invites us to shows closer to the makeup of our scenes in Southeast. After the failed Anaheim show, we are asked to play a high-profile gig at The Smell. Some hybrid punk and drag show to showcase the QTPOC punk community living and breathing on their own terms, curated by a brown nonbinary femme punk who went simply by "Hannah." They caught us playing a blistering set in a Huntington Park backyard, listened to the words through the feedback and the screams: reclaiming space, uplifting voices, death to 45. All that jazz. "Hannah" asked, should we accept the invite to play the punk/ drag show, to tour up and down the coast with their all-brown, all-femme, queercore-punk band, Basura Brujas. We confess we only moonlight as a punk band; we're all college professors by day.

"But we can definitely do the hybrid show," I said, elated.

There is no follow up. Flyers for the punk/drag Show distribute on social media without Pipebomb!'s name anywhere. Sets are set in stone. We waited for their confirmation, but don't want to pry because we want to be good allies. Two of us definitely "POC," none of us have a "Q" nor a "T." Truly, we'd take up space on the bill anyway. I try not to think about hierarchy in this moment, if I am a good ally.

We learn later there is no animosity in the exclusion—"Hannah" simply forgot to reach out. Too bad. The hybrid punk and drag show is a hit. The three of us visit as spectators, seeing the venue claustrophobic with punks of every shade and size and expression. In the end, the show is headlined by a local LA hardcore band consisting of four straight men and a female lead singer—all of whom were allies, all of whom were white.

In Bend,] in front of us stands a bald, white punk with a ragged "God Save the Queen" Sex Pistols shirt—the shirt itself off-white with a Union Jack splayed under the images. His crossed arms covered in more tattoos than mine, though faded and gray from age.

He yells, "I thought this was a punk show? What's with the flowers?" as though the tight torn leather pants squeezed the words out of his torso, not a single syllable in a British accent like his shirt promised. We ignore the white punk and play. We never start with "1, 2, 3, 4s" like the Ramones have you believe. Yacht hits his snare once before belting out blast beats like bullets, Duck's bass rumbles tremors into the parlor's linoleum as my guitar fuzz become furious ocean waves crashing into everyone. Now, the flowers on my buttoned shirt are ferocious.

People react, for better and worse.

Mosh pits flare for the rest our set; the Black and brown kids even feel safe to unglue themselves from the walls. In the cacophony, some hop off tables. Others climb over my amplifier to jump into the crowd. This is the energy we live for—back home, movement is mandatory; the punks exorcise demons in the dance circles, finding each other's rhythm. When songs end, some scream, "More!" Others scream, "Fuck me up!" to fill silence between songs their cocaine brains can't stand. None of this is the polite applause of empty bars. This is the earthquake that shatters buildings built by old money, the master's tools smelted into a language we use to speak over white tongues. For thirty minutes, we are the loudest band on the planet.

Adrenaline keeps my body warm after the set in twenty-degree weather. Sweat soaked through clothes, but we load equipment back into the rental van while accepting hugs from punks who stop us to say they loved our set. Two Black punks are especially glowing from the show, sweat glistening through their pink G.L.O.S.S. and white Death Grips shirts. We swap moisture through embrace, and they go on about how great it was to see an old Black punk in their scene. I am twenty-seven and light-skinned.

"Old?" I ask, nearly saying, "Black?" [Luckily, I have learned better to not talk, not to complicate the community with whatever bullshit grad school fed me. My tongue slipped at the punk/drag show. Surrounded by a utopic community of punks, where donations accrued bail funds for friends, where DIY merch was made on the spot, where Pipebomb! came to support and were welcomed despite our slot on the bill falling through from miscommunication, I still found myself on my academic bullshit. One band had a mindful Black singer who started one song with, "This shit is for *all* my fellow colored people who are targeted by pigs every fuckin' day," which got positive cheers by everyone but me.

"Why is it problematic?" Black punk asked after his set, all my praise for his music extinguished when I pointed to his banter.

"Because 'colored people' is antiquated and offensive, especially toward Black people."

"My dad says 'colored people' all the time. He's Black. He's *been* through some shenanigans, too. How can he be offensive toward Black people?"

"I'm not saying your dad is offensive, it's just not a widely accepted term."

"Okay, then what the fuck do we gotta say?"

"People of color."

"That's the same thing."

"It's actually quite different. You see . . . "

"You throw in the word 'of' and it makes 'colored people' sound less like 'nigger'? Who makes these rules?"

"Look—trust me: the phrase 'people of color' is doing work."

"But *why* is 'colored people' bad when 'people of color' literally uses the same words?

"Because . . . because . . . because . . . "] I take the praise and smile quietly so that the Black punks can hold their joy as they walk back into the pizza parlor. We finish loading our things, readying ourselves to see the next band. I tie my hair into a ponytail to better see where I'm going despite the warmth they could offer from the cold. For once, I want to see faces, and I want mine to catch the chill of the Oregon cold—wishful, I guess, knowing the adrenaline hugging my veins meant the frost would fail. Even though the heat of our bodies staves off the wind, I know it won't last long, so I find a sweater. I hold it in my hands as we close the van doors. Still, I am warm. Between the punks of color staying for us, and seeing all the whites bow to our music, I am frightened by how wide I smile.

"Hot damn! That half-nigger can shred!" the bald, white punk says with an entire chest. He is by the entrance door washed into a group who nervous laugh his words away. [If you are Black—even, or especially, partially Black, you will pause. In the air of this pause is the disbelief that what you heard is what you heard. The dull, naive voice in your head will shriek, "It is (insert any year after 1865), this can't still be happening!" Once that voice quiets, the reminders wash back in: don't wear your hair too nappy or dreaded in a nice restaurant unless you want patrons staring at you the entire meal, don't listen to rap music with the windows down unless you want people to think you're ghetto, don't be a "full-nigger."

If you are not Black, or even a ~~colored person~~ person of color, you may want to be the hero, the ally pulling oppressed bodies out of fires. Sometimes, this helps. Other times, some would say "most" times, this feels like keeping score in hopes to win a trophy, making your heroics tangible.

Ally: Look at the white punk with some semblance of disgust. Shake your head and continue what you're doing. (+1 point) Or, film the white punk, post it somewhere on social media, hope that Shaun King sees it, steals the footage, gets the white punk fired from whatever six-figure job he pretends to hate. (+5 points) Or, tattle to an employee or manager or booker. Don't be afraid to emphasize, "this person is using the n-word like she's talking to David Duke!" (+3.5 points)

Note: If you literally say, "the n-word" rather than "nigger," that's +4 points. However, if you say, "nigger" as in "that white person just called that Black person a nigger, we gotta do something!" and that gets them moving faster through the sheer shock of hearing the word in their vicinity, forcing them to be a witness . . . +4 points. If you relish "nigger" in the previous sentence, don't feel its venom, and instead feel a sudden surge of power you've never felt before courses through your body, you lose all points.

If you are afraid of the latter slipping out, let your Black or brown bandmates guide you this time. Or,] Yacht rushes the white punk; I see his hand struggle to not become a fist, to not make the punk's eye black. Yacht vomits profanities louder than slurs—lets the punk know his language is violence. The other white punks look on in confusion, the wallflowers look with optimistic fear. For a moment, the parking lot is completely quiet, the white punk's mouth agape, holds his hands out like he's had enough—not defeat, but annoyance. Says, "Ok! Ok!" while waving goodbye and serenely walking back into the venue. Duck and I watch, frozen inside the van, my locks tied to watch the whole scene. My muscles tell me to tag in, let Yacht's voice take a rest, but Duck simply says, "Fuck that foo," says we'll have "better shows after this," and that déjà vu holds me back from a fight I can't win. [This is Yacht's victory. Look at his scoreboard. +1,619 Points. A *real* punk motherfucker.

Watch his cape flap in the Podunk Oregon wind. Look around; see everyone where they were before the fight. See nothing change. No applause for sticking up for ~~colored people~~ ~~people of color~~ Black people in absentia.

Now see Yacht inert, maybe coming to, maybe waiting for approval—a real punk motherfucker who wants to give a shit,] but then a friend of Yacht, a different white punk who got us this gig, swears it was a compliment. "Nigger" is a good word, Yacht's friend argues. Like Patti Smith said. The two exchange more words, but one verbal arm twist later, Yacht's friend runs into the venue to tell the white punk it was "not cool" to say that. "Not cool." Imagine a racial slur being put on the same pedestal as out-of-season shoes.

Suddenly, it is cold again.

Inside, I stand at the back of the parlor with the other brown and Black punks, telling myself it's solidarity. Duck joins Yacht in the mosh pits for the next band, deciding against standing with me and the other ~~colored~~ wallflowers. My arms are crossed in LA contempt as I observe with the fellow wallflowers. The last band is all white and plays traditional hardcore, all of them wearing the same leather studded clothing as everyone else. The reaction they receive is bigger than ours. Relentless mosh pits swing fists and boots. Some grab the singer's microphone to scream out-of-sync gibberish. A chair catches fire from a purposeful BIC lighter, then punks leap over the flame like a ritual. At the end, the band wrecks their equipment: guitar necks snap against amplifiers, cymbals slash snare heads. The bassist throws his instrument in the air, knocking loose a piece of ceiling that collides with another punk's skull. The bass itself cracks the ground, the punk bleeds to the rhythm of cheers and cheers and cheers.

The wallflowers say nothing, voices trapped in the maelstrom of white chaos; even their hands go mute when it is time for applause. Mine crawl to the top of my head to undo the locks; they fall over my face like prison bars, but they cloud the cheers from my ears like the moon hiding the sun from earth. This is how we live, anyway—within static where our voices should be so clear, but white noise consumes all the good sound.

They pretend to care about us[, then pretend to be us].

Act II

Three years ago, on an afternoon plane home from Portland, I met my husband Moose. He introduced himself with his real name after our plane almost crashed, but told me he preferred "Moose" after we landed. During that flight, we sat toward the back of the plane where the turbulence hit the worst. An empty middle seat separated us. He slept with his head pressed against the window, wearing black from top to bottom. Hid in the dark from all the white folk losing their patience in the plane. To be fair, we all should have been on the flight a day prior, but that got canceled due to a lingering storm meteorologists swore would end "soon."

They offered comped rooms to a few people, but I opted to stay in the airport so older folk would have somewhere comfortable to rest. I only needed two seats to sleep, successfully cramming my things under both seats, putting my neck pillow to work. Throughout the stay, I watched people come and go from different flights, wondering where their final destinations might be before never seeing them again. I managed a couple hours of sleep before the rescheduled flight but kept waking up thinking something was clawing at my feet. Every time, just a breeze. Every time, I hoped it wasn't a predator, tried not to believe it was a ghost.

The rescheduled plane had been delayed a few times, too: first, a late flight prior to ours congested air traffic, then issues with the wings. We were allowed on after the third delay, but gabachos still got short with the flight attendants as though personally wounded by the wait. One white woman, in particular, told an attendant, "You're making us all late," which would have irked me more if the Asian man behind her didn't roll his eyes for me. When the attendants came around, I made sure to feed them with "thank yous." Often, I pick up the pieces left by white anger when it's not my job—someone has to console the Black and brown workers tens of thousands of feet in the air. Moose says it is a symptom of being an ethnic studies professor; making sure people don't fade away even if it means I do.

I had spent the weekend at an American Studies conference to present my book on Chicana punk, *We Don't Need the English: Fighting Nazi Punks with Black and Brown Hardcore*, to a room full of white women. At every panel, I wore my hair down—natural, raven, curly. My lobes dripped with gold hoop earrings. Sundresses all different shades of loud purple hugged me. Then I wrapped it all in a black denim vest with pins and punk patches stitched all over. A cocoon of my truest self, sutured by my own hands. My doctorate is a piece of paper with my birth name—passed down from Aztec ancestors—scrawled in medieval font. Forever in colonizer's ink, I just prefer to go by my high school nickname even in professional settings.

"Turtledove," they'd say, respect clinging to every letter like they were the ones printed on the degree. I spoke three times, one panel for each day, and received a standing ovation in every room. The first round nourished me, made me feel as though the chair I sat in was truly reserved for my body. By the last talk, my throat felt dry. In the sea of hands, I saw very few Black or brown fingers, limbs my words hoped to unmake as phantoms. Regardless, I took my flowers and left.

In the airport on my way home, I packed my vest into my carry-on since I knew the studs would never make it past the metal detectors. Once I made it to my gate, I pulled out the denim and slipped it over my purple hoodie, which fit over my tied-up hair. By the time the plane hit the sky, the sun had gone down. Moose, who had been asleep since before takeoff, started to stir, but pretended to fall back asleep when the attendants came by to ask if we needed refreshments.

"They leave you alone if you're asleep," he told me a year later, reminiscing after he proposed. "Plus, I didn't want to bother you by reaching over for ginger ale or some shit."

Eventually the attendants finished their rounds. Moose stayed awake, staring out the window. From my view, past his face, I saw clouds beneath us like linoleum, and stars painted over a darkened blue sky slipping into a deeper black—I felt small, a pebble in the quiet of space. Unbothered by detritus, surrounded by the comforting nothingness.

The turbulence in the first twenty minutes of the plane ride helped me adjust to sways, but being in the back still made me believe our section of the plane would tear off after just the right shake. Two small glasses of ginger ale made a decent distraction, then I read what I could for a lecture I needed to give the next day.

Moose peeled away from the window, looked at the book in my lap, his arms still crossed, his body still caved into his black clothing. His mouth opened for a moment, an attempt at communication or an aborted yawn—who knows—the turbulence shook his jaw shut. The shakes were much more violent, and the lights inside the cabin flickered. The flight attendants ran to their seats as the pilots' distorted mumbles soundtracked seatbelt signs lighting up like emergency flares. Before the announcement finished, the plane fell.

The clouds suddenly hovered above our plane. Oxygen masks dropped in front of our faces as our butts hovered above the seats. I let go of my book and gripped my vest: the safety of holding myself under the threat of a crash. A reflex leftover from my younger punk days, uneasy around strangers at late night shows, trying to temper some residual stressors from even earlier in life. "Better than blankets," I always say. My vest in my palms is the best coping mechanism I have to ground myself when I've given too much of myself away. I closed my eyes. A struggling engine echoed in the dark, but I tried to bring the stars back in the blackness, lights to elucidate safety. Then the noise stopped, and the rattle shifted to an upward push. The pilot's muffled messages came through clearer, and I opened my eyes to see Moose's fingers holding my armrest, seeking my attention. His eyes red with water, a tear streaked along his right cheek. He wore the psychotic smirk of a second chance.

"Are you okay?"

*　*　*

I punched a Klan member and was arrested for it, something Moose and I talked about waiting for our baggage claim's carousel to activate after the flight. The topic first came up as we chatted to get our minds off the plane's dip. He was a professor, too, at a community college not far from the university where I teach. Snuck his favorite books into the curriculum, fit in time to play in his punk band, Pipebomb!, with his other professor friends.

Moose had just started full time after years of adjuncting, so he was already unhappy.

"Diversity hire," he said. "I check off both Latinx and Black boxes. The chair told our office assistant, 'Make sure your Lenny-Kravitz-looking adjunct friend with the dreads applies to the call.' Our office assistant is Cambodian and also hates white people, yet the white faculty feel safe around him. Told me once he pretends to be a model minority to trick them into divulging their secrets. That is just one of the things he got told by white higher ups. Neither of us ever feel bad talking shit most days I'm in the office. I go home and play music, and he goes home to skateboard in an abandoned parking lot with friends."

Moose talked more about the disappointments and vitriol he shared with his Cambodian ally, but he had just come from playing a show near Portland, and I wanted to hear about the set. All he said was, "The crowd was pretty cool," and refused a single word more on the subject. We landed, taxied, walked to baggage claim together and took turns getting lost, intoxicated on the stability of walking on solid ground.

Gabachos clamored around the conveyor belt, but Moose and I talked about how our lives intertwined without us noticing. He was born a year after me in a city directly next to my hometown. We went to a lot of the same backyard shows in high school while just missing each other—he had queer friends who brought him to my circles, and I caught all the Black and brown punk bands he ran with. We ate at the same taquerias, studied at the same libraries, recited bad poetry at the same coffee shop open mics. Never once did we speak or make eye contact until our plane fell out of the sky. Creator angry neither of us took the hint.

At the belt, Moose passed some time naming every band on my vest, telling me about the first time he had seen the band live, apologizing every few names for "talking too much." Apologizing for the nostalgia. But I wanted him to keep going, making my punk adolescence and studies feel visible. Wanted to remind him how we're allowed to show off that we exist and continue to exist.

For a long time, the belt did not move. Gabachos tried to get to the front to grab their luggage first and leave. Their claws irritated me; my feet pointed their direction, ready to confront them if they knocked over the Asian couple minding their business in front of the belt. I spent my youth looking out for femmes and people of color in mosh pits; using my small shoulders to protect their bodies from sharpened white elbows, yelling at macho white boys ruining good music with their boots stomping on our toes. I preferred to wear the bruises because I needed to be a shield; I can't bear to see someone else disappear into black and blue.

The white woman from before pushed the Asian man from before to get to the front of the carousel—I wondered if this was revenge for his rolled eyes. He looked unbothered, but still glared at her as though attempting to sear her skin. People mumbled. The aftermath of the shove became a painting; a murder of spectators gathered to analyze the colors on the canvas—they did not touch the art, only stared. Made the Asian man an object.

"Whatever, bitch," he said to small gasps.

"Fuck you, chink," she said.

Louder gasps, a wave of boos. Outrage a placebo for action, as the commotion was the only weapon used to displace her. Regardless, she pressed closer to the carousel, her knees touching the metal as it moved. Her eyes glued to the bags that belonged to the crowd who meant nothing to her. No drops of sweat, no shakes, no stuttered breaths. This woman was unbothered, and I hated her for it. In retaliation for her comfort, for the crowd's comfort, I got loud. I shouted my fancy PhD lingo for a second before showering her with expletives. In response, she stuck her middle finger in the air.

"White devil," I roared. Of all the words I turned into knives, these cut the woman the deepest. She turned around to find my mouth, a golden necklace with Jesus dead on the cross now plainly visible as it swung with her momentum. I hopped up and down to make sure she saw me. I wanted her to shed her skin completely and fight, I wanted to siphon her hatred from the Asian man and onto me. She started taking off a shoe and reeling her arm back to throw it, but the Asian man caught her arm before the projectile launched. A Black security guard intervened to keep the peace. The Asian man and the white woman shouted at one another with the guard in the middle, his eyes locked with the Asian man's exasperated face, his back turned to the violent gesticulations of the woman's clenched fists.

* * *

Four blocks from my university, within view of my office window, a Klan rally marched along the boulevard, chanting "White Lives Matter." Permits be damned, my colleagues and a few of my students launched a counterprotest, making certain the Klan saw a wall of the unafraid. Most of the Klan members were men, or blonde middle-aged women like Airport Woman. We stood face-to-face without touching. A Black cop shouted warnings into the sky as the scorn boiled, hand on holster, sunglasses hiding guilt in his eyes for being paid to defend white hoods. Then a white man dressed in a black polo shirt—confederate flag stitched on the sleeve—swung a giant American flag at one of my students; a Black kid who grabbed the flag and tried to wrestle it away. The tip of the pole adorned with an Eagle statue; the beak sharp enough to penetrate my student's abdomen where the Klan member jammed the staff amid the struggle. When I saw my student fall to the floor, blood coating his palms, I ran to the scene. Instinctually, I punched the white man. After a few moments of bedlam, only me, my bleeding student, and a few colleagues found ourselves in zip ties. I looked up to see the Black cop become a wall between our prone bodies and the Klan members; his face stone, his breaths steadied. Not one Klan member saw jail time.

After the story, Moose and I waited outside the airport for our respective rides. He invited me to a Pipebomb! show the following week in "some dude's backyard in Southeast LA"; the lineup included a couple of queercore bands and a punk act from Tijuana. I had never accepted an invitation so swiftly in my life.

The backyard simmered with punks: brown, Black, queer, Indigenous, old, young, some whites who knew their place. My denim vest kept me warm, as did my black Selena shirt. Pipebomb! had just started, and a mosh pit kicked up dust into the sky like smoke signals. The few white men at the show stood back as everyone else joined the dance circle. A large "ABOLISH ICE" banner haloed the band, and I saw Moose strum with wrath, his chest coated in a rose patterned button up, his dreadlocks exploding in the air like fireworks. I watched my research come to life, watched the summer evening reanimate my youth, watched the mosh pits prioritize the safety of the dancers. People fell, and the music did not continue until the fallen found their feet and started dancing again. I felt a shove, a Black femme with bright pink septum piercing and white lipstick. They smiled wide, as though trying to illuminate a path into the pit with their teeth. They launched themself into the pit, disappearing into the maelstrom of joy. I followed; skanked, pogoed, screamed lyrics I did not know with ferocity as though I did, knowing I would know the words one day. All the freedom in the whirlwind, freedom from the violence of flailing white limbs. Community breathing as the music ate up the sky. Even the stars knew the dance.

Moose and I shared our first hug, his body dripping with sweat, my sweat accented with other people's sweat from the pit. I gripped hard to affirm a thank you, for allowing me an excuse to step outside of academia and return to my hometown for a good pit. Then the cops showed up. White this time. People knew the protocol:

- If this is not your house, do not talk to the cops.
- Kill the noise. Kill the lights. Kill the libations if there are any.
- Freeze.
- The show runner, or the closest in proximity to the property's deed, may speak to the cops if they choose.
- If the show shuts down, it shuts down.
- Do not talk to the cops.
- Do not consent to searches.
- Everyone, in unison, must demand to speak to a lawyer if things turn sour.
- Do not talk to cops.
- We are all witnesses.

Moose's drummer, a white guy, immediately broke the first rule. Stepped up to the cop and ran down the reasons no laws were being broken. Folks were okay with this rule break, especially the "some dude" who actually owned the backyard, considering the unwritten rule of these house shows in Southeast LA: if you've got white privilege to spare, you're on the frontlines. The cop looked past the drummer, stared into Moose and the bassist like a hex, then issued a warning before leaving. The next band started up and we didn't hear from another cop that night.

* * *

Moose and I have matching tattoos on our ring fingers. We agreed it'd be cheaper than engagement rings, lying to ourselves in saying this was solidarity with the communities we grew up with who couldn't afford much and still can't. When the actual wedding came around, we sprung for expensive wedding bands, easily affordable with the full time jobs we'd been privileged with at relatively young ages. Moose won't even be thirty until tomorrow.

Tonight, we celebrate. It's the only chance I'll have, as another conference will pull me away from home for the weekend. So, tonight, only good things. Especially needed after today's class. I lectured on white fragility and the practices needed for allies to feel like accomplices to the plight of the oppressed. Easy stuff. My few white students nodded and took notes as I spoke. Half the queer students of color sat starry eyed hearing their truths validated. The other half tuned out, disinterested in being told about traumas they already knew firsthand. One student, a cishet white guy who makes it a point to talk about each and every protest and organizing meeting he attends in explicit detail, wore a face of confusion throughout my lecture, his hand struggling to stay on the desk. No matter, I kept talking, allowing for dialogue when it felt natural.

"Susan B. Anthony woulda been another white woman taking selfies at the Women's March," one of the queer Black femmes said. Most of us laughed; CisHet did not.

"We are disparaging important women," he said. "Susan B. Anthony was white, so we discredit her historical sacrifices for women's suffrage? You should all feel lucky she ever existed. You should all feel lucky the Women's March even happened."

The two students went back and forth—I wanted them to be able to air their grievances, not to feel I took any of their agency away. I hate that this job has taught me, unfortunately, that some-times a student must lose; if not them, then the professor. After a small pocket of quiet, I recite a failure of Susan B. Anthony's, to be interpreted however the students wish.

I will cut off this right arm of mine
before I demand the ballot for the Negro and not the woman.

CisHet collected his things and stormed out of the classroom. I watched the door in case he made a dramatic re-entrance, but the rest of my attention was directed toward safeguarding my remaining students.

Then they left. I packed my things, erased the board, shut down the computers, shut down the projector, attempted to close the blinds. The university is a few miles away from a small airport in the city. Low flying planes constantly pass by my class's window. Through the window, I saw a 747 pass above campus. I stopped. It exited my sight, and I searched the sky to make sure it didn't come back. I closed the blinds and called Moose as I walked across campus to my car. Of course, we talk lovingly on the phone, but he knows these phone calls make me feel protected when I walk alone; a witness, just in case I'm out of pepper spray.

My feet soak in an orange glow at sunset, a path home before dusk. This semester, our schedules aligned: we are able to finish teaching together and to be home together, to make food together and decompress together. Over the phone, I insist on making dinner for his birthday, shoot down his immediate refusals. There is laugh-ter, like in every call. But in my peripheral vision appears a familiar white specter. A cop? Airport Woman? A disgruntled student from semesters ago—maybe moments ago? It stalks my footsteps slowly, from afar, like a starving leopard in the snow. Moose and I keep talking; I switch to headphones to free my hands: one hand holds my denim, the other readies the cat-shaped keychain (something I bought from a young mujer at a swap meet: ears are sharpened, eyes gaped to fit over my knuckles beautifully for late-night walks to a car) that guards my keys.

Every few seconds, I look over my shoulder. There is wind, and not much else, but I still feel teeth could start nipping at my feet at any moment. I let out a sound—a laugh, a cleared throat, an "um" to bridge a thought I pretend to muster—all to assure Moose nothing is wrong on this walk to the car. He and I both know he will worry too much, so he tells me a joke to try and keep higher spirits. A joke a friend of his told him years ago that made Moose laugh—he says he never got to tell his friend how much it made him laugh.

This woman is playing a serious game of Blackjack. Is on her last few dollars. She's not religious but decides this is the time to start praying. God answers her. Says, "On the next hand, you must hit, my child." She'd dealt a 5 and a 2. She hits. Gets a 7. God says, "On the next hand, you must hit, my child." She hits, gets a 6. She's at 20. She needs an ace. Feels it's too risky. But God says, "You must hit, my child. Trust in me." She hits. Gets a 5. She busts at 25. God says, "FUCK!"

I am in my car forcing laughter. One hand furiously pressing the button to lock the car doors every time I settle into too comfortable of a silence, while my other hand remains wrapped around the cat keychain: my "push to start" car doesn't need the keys in the ignition. I force more laughter. My side mirrors show me nothing. Moose asks if I am okay, asks about my breathing. It picked up a little bit. I say everything is good, then control my breath. In the rearview, I see the familiar white body walking away from my car. Moose asks if I am okay, this time because I start to say something . . . then trail off. I push the button to start the car and lie. Tell him I am perfectly fine. Tell him I am on my way home. Tell him I have to chop vegetables and put on the chicken. Moose says he will be late: he had to run to the main offices to report an incident in his class. He promises it was nothing bad, that we'll discuss at dinner. We say goodbye; he knows I don't like to drive and talk. I check my rearview more than I look at the road home ahead of me.

Dinner is easy to prepare with all the nice appliances we've accumulated over the years. Our house is in a nice neighborhood with white neighbors we don't talk to, and the yard stretches wide, making us feel far from our hometowns despite how near they are. Inside, we lined the walls with photos of family and friends and shows and trips: a Pan-American flag hangs above the sixty-inch television; a large decorative Sarchi oxcart wheel, gifted by one of Moose's elderly Costa Rican tías, is placed behind our new record player. An altar dedicated to the fallen in my life, adorned with incense, flowers, funeral programs, Velas designed with the Virgen de Guadalupe or San Miguel, and Dia de los Muertos papel picado, stands as tall as our media bookcases stuffed with movies and records and video games and books. Our boarding passes from Portland are framed above our electric stove.

I want to believe our ancestors would marvel at our decorations, and how the colors pop with the celebration of their heritage— though I often wonder if they would even be able to get in through the door without having the cops called on them by our nameless neighbors. If they made it through the door, would the ancestors look at our Limp Wrist poster and know how I failed a stage diver? I look at this poster every day before Moose gets home. The show was our honeymoon present to each another. Moose and I danced in the pit for their show at the Regent in LA, surrounded by queers and folks of color. Then a rainbow-haired brown femme launched herself from the stage, confident she'd land in the safety net of her community. The show had more white boys than I had hoped, slam dancing and shoving people around, sacrificing dance moves for violence. I lost Moose in the crowd for only a moment, but in that time, I saw the femme land headfirst onto the floor, bleeding and possibly concussed. I should have caught her. I wanted to hurt the white boys for their own neglect. I wish Moose hadn't disappeared into the ocean of punks when we needed him. I look at this poster, then my own hands now under the kitchen lights. I see my knuckles shine in a fairer brown.

Moose walks in and plops his work bag by the door; his grimace tells me the office visit did not go well. Still, we kiss, we hug, and we sit down to eat. He tries to get back up, offering to grab extra utensils or warm my food, but I nearly beg him to sit down, to relax, to eat. We are silent for a few minutes—hunger keeps our mouths occupied. I am only halfway through my plate, but Moose has inhaled all his food and guzzled a large glass of water.

"So, there's this Nazi in my class," he says. "He's been in my class, but I figured he was reformed or something. Said he was in prison for thirty years, has this aged swastika flag tattooed on his left forearm—extremely detailed, by the way. I mean, the flaps and the shading clearly took hours, which means he sat there getting poked and *wanting* this tattoo. I'm grossed out by how impressed I was by that ink. Even worse, he's nice. He's one of only a few white students in there and he has an easy time doing groupwork with the others. Talks to me about punk rock all the time before and after classes. I never brought him up because he didn't cause trouble.

"But they turned in their first essay drafts yesterday and I got to his; the topic was paths to social mobility. Most students wrote about equality for education and jobs and shit. This dude wrote a six-page rant about why Mexicans are ruining the country and why border patrolmen need to do better at gunning down 'the wetbacks' to keep our country safe. Even had a section about wanting to beat up classmates for stealing education. I took it to the office because what am I even supposed to do in this situation? The chair looked at the essay, cringed, sighed, then smiled at me and said, 'Well, it's a rough draft. I'm sure this can be fixed after some edits. Besides, you're better at this stuff than I am. That's why we hired you.' He goes back in his office. The office assistant and I looked at each other like, 'I guess we'll just die then.'"

I get up to grab a key lime pie out of the fridge. I collect a Bic lighter and "30"-shaped candles, place them in the center of the pie and light a flame. I fit a green party hat over his dreadlocks, a purple one over my curls. I kiss him on the cheek, I tell him, "You're home now. No Nazis here. You don't have to die tonight," and sing "Happy Birthday." A smile cracks his mouth, his shoulders relax. He closes his eyes before blowing out the flame. We hug again, and I apologize for missing his real birthday tomorrow, for his present arriving late despite how early I ordered it. I want to apologize for his life—having to work with the Nazi, for his department chair, for him and the office assistant's resignation to invisibility. I stop myself, once again, from apologizing for closing my eyes when bodies needed to be caught from the sky.

"Are you excited for the weekend?" he asks with genuine curiosity, gripping my arm. His fingertips vibrate with care. I sit down as we both eat pie; he looks at me, thrilled to listen. For a few moments, I just speak to fill the air, but eventually I start enjoying my words, my successes; traveling to celebrate the milestones I was never meant to achieve in academia, milestones to celebrate ancestors I do not know would approve.

"The next book has a title already," I say. "¡No Importa the Sex Pistols, Aquí Está Pónk!"

"I love it," Moose says smiling. "Weed out the whites."

The laugh I give him is hearty and free, and for once tonight we are both smiling without exertion. Then our laughter is drowned out by the sound of shattering glass. Our alarm system blares. Moose runs toward the noise, then out the door. I chase after him, fast enough to see him on the tail of a white figure—that familiar ghost from earlier—running, the specter's right arm beaming red from cuts along the skin. They both disappear into the night, the dimmed streetlights masking their trail. I see in our front window a perfectly sized hole matching the figure's fists, glass confettied all over our hardwood. For a moment, I consider stopping to pick up the glass, cleaning our home to erase the intrusion, but I don't. My legs keep going until I trip over Moose's workbag, falling onto our stoop. I am on my knees; the air in my lungs explodes out of my mouth, inhaling feels like knives.

I close my eyes and hope for stars, but when I open them, I only see deep night. My peripheral tingles but can't sense any more specters. If I look over my shoulder, the ghosts don't go away; they will throw another brick to shatter me. My black denim armor would scream if it had a mouth as my nails dig into the stitching.

Then my hands start to warm, cupped inside another's. I open my eyes to see the tattoos on our fingers mirroring one another, conjoined in a shared unknown. I squeeze the hand instead of the threads of my vest. Moose has come back; we are now surrounded by white neighbors who don't know our names, but know us now by the broken glass that stains our home. Murmurs of "the police are on their way" swarm in the air. I don't want to talk to cops. I don't need witnesses. But my lungs relent. Exhale. Moose has a cut above his left eye, small but bleeding. A drop falls onto his cheek like a tear, painting his skin a vivid red, proving the wounds are real. He smiles, gripping my hand even harder as though the blood were mine.

The ghost got away. I ask Moose, "Are you okay?" deathly afraid he will say yes.

Act III

Here is Moose: He stands outside the venue to find oxygen not yet staled by the very few bodies who came to see Pipebomb! play a show. He breathes, watches cars pass. The venue is near empty, save for a fistful of friends antsy to go home. It's late. Even the opening band has already left. Moose hears a distant woman say "amor," thinks it's Turtledove. He turns fast in hopes that she made it to the show after all, that her conference got postponed or canceled and the first thing she wanted to do was catch Pipebomb!, but "amor" evaporates into the night air—a passersby with no interest in Moose's punk. Moose settles for Turtledove's text, "Have a great show," sent from a distance, far from the music, far from Moose screaming into a room full of ghosts. Before Moose walks back into the venue, he touches the rose patterns on his shirt while trying to settle nerves in his stomach, disappointed the thorns don't prick his hand.

*

Here is Upper Duck in Pipebomb!'s rehearsal space. First, for once. Blacky Moose and Id y Yacht still on the way. Alone, Duck tends to his corner of the room. The Ampeg SVT-CL is his height, its purple light fading in and out of consciousness; the speakers growl like a bomb, but cough as their light threatens to dim. Duck plugs in the left-handed black and red Ibanez TMB-100 bass—almost new, the replacement for a malnourished Squier broken at some previous show. A pluck. The floor rumbles. The purple blazes. Duck's soles warm.

*

Sometimes, Duck goes to a pond a ten-minute walk from one of his campuses. Actual ducks flock to his feet; his calloused hands tear pieces of bread for their lunch. As an adjunct with other classes to teach at different campuses, Duck spends only brief lunches at the water. If he is done for the day, he'll slip an edible to decompress. Once, early on in his career, a duck sat between his legs after he dosed too much on one such break. He looked down at its head for an entire lunch break, marveling at the flux of its shape. Beginning his next class while still incredibly high, he lectured on the distinct shape of a duck's head from the top. Its transformation into a dog's face, then candy corn: give something enough attention and it will become something else just to spite your vision. The students caught on that Duck was high, teased him in later classes about his lecture on the upper parts of a duck. Professor Upper Duck. Professor Duck. Yo, Dr. Duck. Duck adopts the name when he gigs for punk bands. His students catch on to this, too. Duck is the cool professor. Wears his pins to work. Graf Orlock. Ceremony. The shape of the United States, halved, the southern bits adorned with the Mexican flag and the words "Make America Mexico Again." Duck is a white-presenting Mexican American man, monolingual in English, but he's the cool professor, made cooler by all he must have had to overcome to even stand in front of the class to teach. Sometimes, though he won't admit it, it is his friendship with Moose that makes Duck the coolest professor.

*

Duck and Moose have the same teacher before they ever meet each other. Mr. Kelly, a plump white man, teaches seventh grade math in South Gate. New, meek, wants to reach the children. Wants to become their beacon of hope, to be the one white teacher who doesn't revel in destroying already othered kids. Wants to be their knight. Plus, it doesn't hurt he was promised his student loans would be erased by teaching in a low-income neighborhood. This is his first week out of suburbia. In the first five minutes of class, trying to speak to kids who talk over him, yet not raising his voice no matter how necessary, Mr. Kelly realizes they do not want his help. Normally a good student, even Moose gives Mr. Kelly little attention, instead trying to impress the other kids. Trading jokes and insults as a form of camaraderie, lobbing trash into wastebaskets, saying, "Guess I'm just Costa Rican then," when he misses. By the fourth day, after the class has stopped paying attention to Mr. Kelly completely, going about their business swapping chisme and playing cards, Mr. Kelly tries to send a kid to detention as a warning to the class. The kid punches Mr. Kelly in the gut, laughs, and receives an extra day of detention. Nothing more. Moose misses the actual punch, too busy with a royal flush. Mr. Kelly is transferred to Rosamond where he tries to teach Duck's class algebra, and fails once again. A fire consumes a classroom whole when he can't stop eighth graders from smoking a joint in class.

*

Here come Blacky Moose and Id y Yacht to the rehearsal space, greeted by the rattle of Duck's bass. The hugs are meaty, wet with the sweat bleeding through Duck's Pig Destroyer T-shirt. The moisture of improvement, of Duck loving the newness of his instrument more and more, of becoming proficient so no one will be disappointed in him. Yacht wheels in a dolly carrying his drum set. The cymbals are rust colored, their crash as loud as broken glass. Blue casings chipped from seventeen years of gigs since Yacht first bought them secondhand at age nineteen. The drums wear stickers like bandages. Moose unzips a torn guitar case, pulls out the all-black Fender Telecaster Esquire with the Bigsby tremolo bar. Duct tape cauterizes the input jack. The single pickup on the bridge is loose, but still screams.

*

See Moose's Pops work his security job at Avalon in Hollywood. Bored, him and his coworkers talk of side hustles since there's not a lot of money in this job. One coworker tries to unload a Fender Telecaster, solid black with a Bigsby tremolo bar, onto someone for only a couple hundred bucks. Pops calls Moose, "My buddy is selling this Prince-lookin' guitar. You want it?" Moose's professor paychecks are larger than his Pops' checks, but still only just pay the bills. Moose says, "Let me check my finances first, then I'll let you know," before ending the phone call. Pops thinks, "Fuck that." Next time Moose visits his parents for a Sunday dinner, Pops hands Moose a torn guitar bag with a solid black Fender Telecaster inside. "Haggled with my buddy, got it for a good price. Your punk band will sound better with this Prince guitar."

In person, the guitar has an unapologetically black luster. The fretboard is a maple coat akin to Moose's Mamá's skin. Moose plays it. It feels perfect when his hands dance over the fretboard like a waterfall crashing into a lake to become a whole body; "Pops," Moose wants to say, "Look at this sheen. Goddamn, look at it. Such beautiful Blackness alive within my fingers."

"Pops," Moose actually says. "Thanks."

*

The white strap, never washed, dulled to a dirt brown, is lined with pins from bands made up of friends, local bands that have broken up, an enamel pin of the planet Mercury, an enamel pin of Rocko from *Rocko's Modern Life*, and a warped plastic pin reading "Too Cool for this Planet" from the "Homerpalooza" episode of The Simpsons. Yacht is dressed for work, professional professor attire to sweat all over. Moose is dressed for the show later tonight. Roses kiss the white of his short-sleeve button up, his knees breathe through holes in black jeans. Duck is jealous of the years of love poured into his bandmate's broken instruments. The aged red eruption of Moose's Orange CR120 masks the purple glow of Duck's own light. The windows tremble from feedback. Punk precum.

*

Here, Moose is fourteen or fifteen. Pops calls him into the master bedroom, yelling with the urgency of imminent death. Moose runs inside. On Pops's TV, Prince plays a guitar solo on a yellow Telecaster with leopard print on the pickguard. His erudite fingers pirouette across the fretboard, the notes sing and coat the theater walls. In the background, Tom Petty and Dhani Harrison strum along to The Beatles' "While My Guitar Gently Weeps," and watch Prince with glee. Red fedora, red silk shirt, black suit. Prince plays the solo with such out-of-body, ethereal reverence, Prince transports the Brit boys' rock song down into its Black roots. He falls into the arms of a Black security guard whose own trusting hands swiftly lift Prince back on stage; not a single note missed, he takes up space as though collecting reparations. Prince's voice is the loudest without saying a word.

As though watching Saturday-morning cartoons, Pops lies on the bed with a pillow under his chin, says, "That's how you play guitar!"

The teenage angst fights its way to Moose's mouth, needing to say "whatever," or "this is what you called me in for?" but Prince silences him. Prince's flamboyance exudes dominance, his sensuality commanding respect, his diminutive frame radiating strength, his Blackness proud and potent on screen despite the white audience.

"This is punk," Moose says, an awe and clarity forcing the angst mute.

Pops tells Moose to keep watching Prince, to look at his techniques, his fashion. "This is how a Black man performs," he says, all eyes on his hands. The song ends, the crowd applauds; cameras pan to aristocratic whites sitting at tables weighed down by expensive meals and champagne. Without warning, Prince tosses his guitar off his shoulders for no one to catch, looks away from the falling star before it crashes into the stage. He struts off stage while the white rock stars congratulate themselves for inviting a Black friend to their party.

A standing ovation.

*

Moose teaches English composition full time in Orange County. He hates it. Being a diversity hire, everything he does festers with tokenization. He ties his locks back in a ponytail, but students still assume they can buy weed from him. Fellow faculty come to him for advice they'll never use on "decolonizing their syllabus," asking to prove they can ask. In his early afternoon composition course, two biracial students are enrolled. Some white counselor advised both of them separately to take a younger professor like Moose. Moose gives them affectionate punk names when he speaks about them to others. SkaterBoi and Blaxican. The former a "surf punk" who wears tight, bright tank tops and rolls into class on a longboard until Moose tells him to stop. His head drips with dreadlocks like Moose, only SkaterBoi's are dyed gold down to the roots. Blaxican keeps things simple. A hip-hop head who wears plain T-shirts and shorts to class every day with Adidas sandals and long white socks, music playing from his phone's speakers until Moose tells him to turn it off. Both half Black. Both half brown. Both answer questions in class while everyone else stays silent during discussions. They make fast friends the first day of class, feel emboldened to speak loud in every lecture, having a professor who looks like them and who's close to their age. Moose appreciates it until he doesn't.

*

SkaterBoi is in a punk band, been relentless about getting Moose to see him play. Says, "We both have dreads and Bad Brains shirts, prof! Birds of a feather, right?" Moose is always busy grading, or has family coming in, or has promised his wife a night out—all that personal stuff. Blaxican is less pushy, talks to Moose after class about books, asks for recommendations. This is Blaxican's third try taking composition. He wants to do as well as he can, read as much as he can. He does not want to fail. Moose does not want him to fail, yet fears going so easy on them will be their downfall. He also does not want to be like Blaxican's first instructor. A white guy, even younger than Moose, made sure his whole syllabus oozed with academics of color. Asked Moose for suggestions, then their boss commended White Instructor for such daring book choices. In the end, White Instructor could not get past Blaxican's colloquial grammar, no matter how sound his arguments. He even decided to change entire lesson plans to focus on grammar after grading Blaxican's essays specifically. White Instructor eventually failed Blaxican. Moose does not want to fail Blaxican *or* SkaterBoi. Goes easy on them to avoid failing them. This way, Moose can hide their failures, brag to White Instructor about how much better he is at teaching.

*

Duck was Blaxican's second instructor. Moose doesn't know this, even after getting Duck hired for an adjunct position at his Orange County college. Trusting that Duck would be a good influence for the nonwhite students on campus. Trusting that Duck would break up the monotony of majority-white faculty members talking down to nonwhite students about proper sentence structures. Duck, to his credit, spent a lot of time on Blaxican. Critiqued every line of his essays so the next draft would be perfect. Scrutinized his tests and quizzes more than anyone else's so the next tests and quizzes would be perfect. Asked Blaxican more questions than the other students, hoping his answers would be perfect. Most of the time, Blaxican felt too pressured and too mush-mouthed to elaborate on his thoughts. Duck, regardless, remained glued on Blaxican hoping not to let Moose down: Moose got Duck this job and expects better from Duck—or so Duck assumes. Duck needed Blaxican to succeed. But Blaxican's rewrites still only earned him a D+ on a good day, while other students' papers garnered a B+ or higher. Blaxican's motivation to do better was snuffed with every non-passing grade; he dropped Duck's course before midterms. A week later, another student asked Duck for an extension on an essay. Said her cousin got caught up in gang activity, fatally shot during a drive-by. Still despondent from Blaxican quitting his class, Duck asked the student if her cousin wrote her essays for her. "No? Then no extension."

*

fuck. is SkaterBoi's band's name. Lowercased and you need to have the period. The newest, hottest local punk band making waves—their shows are ebullient exhibitions of youthful destruction. They welcome queerpunks and white skinheads alike. The band is a quartet of punks freshly in their twenties: Black boy drummer, queer white girl guitarist, Afrolatino singer—SkaterBoi—and a white bass player with a rich and connected dad. Local papers write about them with attention and reverence Pipebomb! never knew: "The Afropunk/queercore band we need to drive an adrenaline needle into rock and roll's chest!" Duck hates them. Moose hates them—lies about having plans so he does not have to see his student succeed at being a Black punk in ways Moose never could. Yacht does not know who they are. Duck complains to Pipebomb!: "They literally just have songs about bong rips and surfing. They're changing things in punk? No manches! They play the same damn blast beats as any stupid hardcore band. And they only get shows because the bassist's corpse-lookin'-ass-dad did a bunch of acid with every booker in town and can snap his fingers to get shows with a crowd. They're called, '*fuck.*,' for fuck's sake. How do you even market that?" Regardless, SkaterBoi is proud of *fuck*. Their claim to fame came recently. *fuck.* played inside a closed diner owned by a friend of *fuck.*'s bassist's father. No less than two hundred punks came to the gig and slam danced. Crowd surfers knocked over hanging lights. Band members stood on tables to play their instruments. Punks who couldn't fit inside the diner started mosh pits in the parking lot. When the cops came to shut down the show, they billed the band a reported $1,000 in damages. Moose disdains how brown and Black punks see *fuck.*'s ruinous gathering as anti-capitalistic heroism. Duck ignores their social media, hoping they go away. Both feel a traitorous joy knowing the cops showed up.

*

"We went over 'using music to create an argument,' right? I play a song for them, and they have to tell me if it was good or bad. You know, develop a thesis. 'This is a good song because x, y, and z.' Then they tell me why the song is good or bad by considering the music, the lyrics, and the message. When I play Michael Jackson or Drake, they'll usually tell me the song is good because they've heard it before. Then I play Nirvana. Not 'Smells Like Teen Spirit.' I play 'Tourette's' and watch everyone squirm. It's hilarious. I'll ask, 'Was it a good song?' and a lot of students will say, 'God no!' because the screaming was scary. Today, SkaterBoi said something along the lines of, 'It's a great song because there's hatred and anger. The song is destructive, like how they broke shit at their shows. Destruction is punk as fuck!' In my head I said, 'No, it's not punk as fuck. Purposefully destroying equipment—especially in *this* economy—is irresponsible and a gross display of wealth, and your hard-on for destruction is your colonizer ancestry talking, you dick.' But I just said, 'Great observation,' and moved on.

"Blaxican had a much better answer. He said he didn't like the song, but his thesis was that the song was great. The song performed what the title promised: screaming nonsense. He had taken the time to look up what 'Tourette's' even was and how Kurt Cobain committed suicide. Said it was a perfect song to release anger, not because it was the 'punk' thing to do, but because it seemed like Cobain was everywhere and nowhere, like everyone stared at him but couldn't see him. Then Blaxican said that sometimes it's hard to say things out loud when you're suffering, but playing music that is crazy-ass noise might be the best way to tell someone, 'Hey, I ain't doin' so hot, bro.' He said, 'That's probably why he broke all his shit all the time, too. Just couldn't say how much he hated life.' I literally clapped. No one else did.

"At the end of class, I passed back essays. Gave SkaterBoi an 'F' and Blaxican a 'B+.' Blaxican was stoked. He earned it. Grammar could use work, but goddamn, his arguments were solid. SkaterBoi gave me some last-minute bullshit. Obvious he typed up whatever and submitted it moments before a *fuck. show.* Emailed me that night; just wrote 'bruh, I thot u had me . . . : (' "

*

Hey. Hey. Hey. Hey. Hey! Hey! Hey! Mean heart. Cold heart. Cold heart. Cold heart. Cold heart. Cold heart. Cold heart. Cold heart.

*

Duck thinks about this moment a lot: on a particularly sunny Wednesday, Moose and Duck have lunch together at the pond between classes. The sun beats down on the two punks like a spotlight. Duck threw together turkey sandwiches for each. Packed a couple of day old bolillos for the ducks, too. As he'd promised, lunch was on him. Said he knew Moose's favorite fixins and would make the best damn sandwich he could make. As the ducks float by, ignoring breadcrumbs, Moose says he feels he's doing everything wrong from so many angles: a teacher, a punk, Black, brown. Duck knows Moose is talking, but Duck stops paying attention as his afternoon edible kicks in. When he looks at Moose, he sees sweat dripping from Moose's locks as the sun hits its highest point in the sky. Moose speaks clear as day, but Duck misses the words. Duck waits for Moose's mouth to stop moving. Says, "For sure," when the time is appropriate. Says, "Foo, I just thought of the dopest shit for a song!" Now it's Moose who stops paying attention, bites into his sandwich. Mayonnaise drips off the crust. Moose hates mayonnaise.

*

The first thing Duck says while hugging Moose in the rehearsal space: "Happy birthday, Chulo! Welcome to the dirty thirties." Moose smiles, returns to setting up for practice. Duck, Moose, and Yacht trade jokes and pleasantries, ignoring the pressures of playing a show later in the evening, ignoring concerns of being underprepared to play on Moose's birthday. The mood dips a bit as Duck asks about Moose's morning, if any birthday shenanigans had taken place yet.

"This morning, we had breakfast at my folks' apartment," Moose says, tuning his guitar, not looking up. "A bunch of family showed up. Wasn't expecting that. A couple cousins from Costa Rica are in town. No one told me ahead of time. But I walk in with Turtledove, and everyone yells, 'Happy Birthday!' They strung up a bunch of 'You're 30! Yay!' signs everywhere. Mamá made picadillo empanadas and brewed coffee with Costa Rican coffee beans. So that was tight. Took obligatory pictures with everyone. Turtledove ate it all up, but I wasn't in the mood. Pops asked about the band. I just said, 'It's going fine,' then tried to change the subject to work. I wanted to talk about making sure my students don't flunk out. Figured the family would wanna hear about the part of my life that makes money. But they kept pressing. They wanted to know about the music, reminding me of when I was a teen playing electric guitar in my room for hours and not getting homework done. They laughed about it. I kept cramming empanadas in my mouth so I'd have an excuse to not talk. My cousins asked what kind of music we play. Their English is terrible, so I just said, 'Oh, it's punk.' These cousins are older by at least a decade, but they have nose rings and tattoos and Metallica shirts. One still plays drums for a couple local bands in Costa Rica. They all got excited, started bumping shoulders to mimic mosh pits from their younger days. Sang that 'I am an anti-chrrrist' bullshit that I hate. I kept eating my empanada. Said, 'Is fun to do the, how you say, slam dance.' Then the cousins asked if we were playing anytime soon. Turtledove yelled, 'Estan tocando hoy en la noche!' before I could lie and say no. Luckily my folks planned something different with them tonight. No one told me anything.

"I didn't want them there, anyway. I'm thirty now. Don't need my family seeing me play 'pretend rock star' like a fucking child." The guitar is tuned perfectly.

Moose, tired of talking, plays his guitar. Duck and Yacht follow suit for one hour. Locked inside the safety of rehearsal, Pipebomb! practices a set. At first, they're careful not to destroy their throats, careful not to burn out before people can watch. But Moose's dreads come untied, his and Duck's feet lift off the ground to the pulse of Yacht's drums.

Fuck it. They can't ignore this joy: no folded arms judging from the sidelines, no pretentious white punks comparing their songs to '70s Anglo-heroes, no violence perpetrated with their music as a soundtrack. Nothing to prove. They're alone in the practice room, but they all pretend the show is happening now. The celebration of Moose's thirtieth year of existence starts. They imagine a mosh pit as a rainbow of pogoers singing along to Moose's verses and Duck's screams. Neither their voices nor their instruments disintegrate. The men swap sweat expelled by divine fury, the music pushing their age and disappointments out of the room. Duck notices his own presence within the music for what feels like the first time—nothing in his body to numb the moment like usual; his booze still in the mini-fridge, his weed still free from fire, his brownies uneaten. Duck smiles inside the heat, the sharp melodies carved by his brothers' tools. Duck feels invincible. Duck is the cool professor who will play a perfect set tonight.

*

Duck, on his way to the venue, pulls over to read this message from one of the opening bands: "Hey dawgs, so sry to do this but we haveto drop out of the show. *fuck*. ask us to play their show tonight and we couldnt say no. u get it tho right" Duck sits in his car, parked on the shoulder of a busy freeway, reads this online article from SPIN: "Local L.A. punk band, *f***.*, started a GoFundMe page to pay for damages accrued during their breathtaking DIY diner show. Many felt it unfair and unnecessary to charge these teenagers and college students such a steep bill. Yet, just as they were about to reach their $1,000 goal, Bay Area punk icons Green Day donated an extra $2,000 to their cause. They left the following note: *Hey f**** [redaction ours], *Call us! We want to play the Bastard's Club with you. Love, Green Day.*" Duck finishes the article, tries to escape seeing all the praise and solidarity by closing the page and scrolling through social media to reset himself.

But Duck sees *fuck.* has posted something moments ago. Over-joyed by the visibility, celebrating their newfound mainstream appeal of being "the band bailed out by Green Day," fuck. announced "*a surprise local show. 2NITE!!!! Hella f***en stoked 2 see ever1 loose there sh** in the pit 1 mo' 'gain!!'*" 2NITE!!!! is tonight. Duck pulls off the shoulder and continues his drive to the venue. He does not tell Moose nor Yacht what he'd read.

*

Watch Mr. Kelly get fired from his second-chance teaching gig at Rosemond for "failing to stop a student from setting fire to a classroom." Watch Duck say nothing as the Black kid is hauled away, expelled; Mr. Kelly collects his office belongings. Watch Duck say nothing, knowing his roach caused the fire, falling out of his clumsy fingers, catching the dry carpet. The Black kid, as a matter of fact, was the only person to try and put out the flames. Watch Duck struggle to say "sorry" to the Black kid, who heard nothing before being taken away—after all, Duck would need to remember the Black kid's name first, and he can't even do that.

*

Moose inputs final grades for the composition class he hates. SkaterBoi does not pass. SkaterBoi walks out of the final; an in-class essay based on a book he did not try to read, expecting Moose to take mercy on him. Instead of text, SkaterBoi draws a lightning bolt striking the DC capital building, hoping Moose might smile. "Sit back down and write a real damn essay," Moose says, receiving the final, glancing at the drawings, then staring daggers into a smiling SkaterBoi waiting at Moose's front desk for an A.

"Why? I didn't even read that shit." So Moose draws a giant F in red ink.

SkaterBoi starts to leave but decides to shove Moose's bag off the front desk, knock over the podium. Passing papers float in the air like loose feathers of a freshly shot bird. SkaterBoi—proud, accomplished, a real punk motherfucker—skates out of the class. Moose doesn't flinch. The class murmurs in fear. Blaxican freezes, but his pen stays kissing his paper. Blaxican stays in his seat, not only for his education but to avoid disappointing Moose. *The solace of representation,* Moose thinks, as the disaster of representation crushes his shoulders.

*

A feather floats in a pond, detached from a duck's body. The sun bleeds through a magnifying glass to take the life of an ant.

*

Duck wants to rework the set. Make it longer. They deserve the extra time. It's Moose's birthday. "Don't worry about the other bands," Duck says. Another opening band forfeits sharing a stage with Pipebomb! in favor of seeing *fuck*.'s set. Duck has yet to tell Moose or Yacht. Duck just wants this set to be perfect. Maybe students will come. Duck, after all, announced to all of his classes across all of his campuses that he was playing a show. Free advertising makes up for the adjunct life, he figured. Duck is the cool professor. Duck does not know that the few students who would have showed, instead, will see *fuck*. to mourn SkaterBoi's academic future. Duck does not know SkaterBoi sees Moose's heart as mean and cold. Does not know SkaterBoi wants Moose exiled from punk; will take the stage screaming FUCK MOOSE. Screaming RACE TRAITOR. Screaming COLONIZER. SkaterBoi's golden dreads swinging like pendulums, pocket watches hypnotizing young punks to slam dance, shoulders bruised by elbows, elbows becoming knives stabbing haphazardly in the dark.

*

Here is Moose: back inside the venue, walking up to the rest of Pipebomb! who are ready to play. Moose picks up the black Telecaster. Moose does not see Yacht stare at him, concerned that Moose has not said a word. Moose does not see Duck, drunkenly talking with the remnants of the crowd. Says, "We're Pipebomb! y'all," to the crowd of seven, then six. "Today, our guitarist, Blacky Moose, turns thirty. Let's make this a motherfuckin' ripper in his honor!"

Duck turns to Moose with Cheshire teeth. Says, "Let's play, Blacky." Duck and Yacht launch into the first song; Moose can't even hold a pick. No one notices. The barflies drink. Eyes drift. A purple light gives Duck's amp life. It blinds, an amethyst supernova,

59

then fades. The buzz lulls to a mumble then dies. Duck stumbles over to see what is wrong. His drunk hands stumble over knobs. Halfway through the song, he plays his dead bass as though he had resuscitated its sound. No one notices. Thinks it's all part of Pipebomb!'s set. Bob their heads arrhythmically to the dying noise. Now, an old white couple at the bar pays attention. Silent when Duck said it was Moose's birthday, they cheer Duck's inebriation, raise a glass to his disaster.

"Now *this* is punk," they scream, salivating over the faults.

Yacht struggles to keep playing the dying song, but his rhythms are steady as Moose and Duck spiral. The bass has completely disappeared, then Moose's guitar mutes. He unslings the Telecaster, relieving the guitar's weight from his defeated shoulder. There are only drums. They race like palpitations as Yacht keeps going. Hopes his bandmates will follow his lead. But Moose grips the Telecaster's maple neck and surrenders its black body, the descendant of Prince's punk, to destruction. Moose slams the body of the guitar onto his amp with the force of a baseball bat. Knobs fly off. The power dies. The Costa Rican flag hung over the amp's face tears down the middle after a second swing. Yacht keeps drumming through the disembowelment, and Duck strums his bass emitting complete silence. Now the whole bar pays attention. Moose swings the guitar again, a fourth time. The body snaps, collides with his face.

Blood saturates Moose's dreadlocks, blends into the roses. Moose swings faster. The body breaks completely. He throws the guitar neck across the bar. Top shelf booze shatters. The neck bounces; strings cut the old white woman's cheek. Her husband looks at Moose, wants to cut him tenfold for what he has done. But the old white woman stops him. She applauds. Then he applauds. Then the bartender, the three leftover audience members.

"Encore! Encore!"

Here is Pipebomb! disarmed: blood fixes a crimson mask over Moose's face. Duck finally unplugs his broken instruments. Yacht stops drumming, leaves his seat, hugs both men as tight as he can, wants them to feel held, wants to lead them away from the stage lights. Neither Moose nor Duck move. Neither hear Yacht say, "It's gonna be fine, guys. It's gonna be fine." Moose's blood soaks blisters on Yacht's palms, and Duck cries into Yacht's shoulders. Applause sustains, grows shriller. Moose stares at what is left of the broken Prince Telecaster Pops never saw him play; the Costa Rican flag shredded underneath the smoldering pile of black shrapnel.

Moose looks up, blinded by stage lights, and does not see the standing ovation.

Ballads and Balisongs

The bar in the heart of their hometown stinks of their teen years. Mezcal and Machista cologne smears the walls, but this is where Munkey wanted to meet Moose. They have not spoken in over a year, having missed each other's weddings for reasons both legitimate and embellished. Moose approaches the entrance, still unsure how to think about Munkey's sudden invitation. Still, Moose—almost embarrassingly so—remains hopeful that this invitation is as wholesome as their friendship used to be before El Paisa.

Two weeks prior to this meeting, both Moose and Munkey found out a mortar had killed El Paisa while on tour in Iraq. Moose's parents forwarded him an obituary, asking if it was the same friend from high school, to which Moose lied, "No." But when Munkey got the news that he had lost one of his best friends forever, heard from the remnants of his hometown friend circle, he immediately broke down. Out of fear that time would take Moose away as well, Munkey reached out for a drink or two to catch up. Moose obliged, figured at worst he loses an evening, at best he rebuilds some bridges with Munkey.

Both felt, after all, they could benefit from undoing the guilt of prolonged silence. When Moose walks in, Munkey waves him down to the bar stools where he has two tall IPAs in front of him—the sweatier one waiting for Moose—and an empty shot glass waiting to be bussed. Through the hall of old Mexican men drunkenly belting "Volver, Volver" to the heavens, through the tables of cholos speaking brash Spanish and eating hot wings, Moose maneuvers toward his old friend and wears a cautious smile even as they hug.

Men in the bar give the two quick glances, brief judgment of their hug, some curious stares for their fashion, which is more vándalo than everyone else's caballero chic. Nevertheless, they embrace to feel the best parts of their past return to their fingertips. Moose feels the denim of Munkey's jacket, the giant patch of Megadeth's *Rust in Peace* album cover stitched to the back, the "hecho en Mexico" eagle sewn into the shoulder. When they pull away, Munkey accidentally tugs off both the "ACAB" and Prince enamel pins on the lapel of Moose's aged leather jacket. Moose reattaches them as Munkey apologizes, complimenting Moose's now neck-length dreadlocks to extinguish any hints of Moose's annoyance. Both men sit down, facing one another, and cheers in celebration of finally making this hangout happen.

Moose chokes down the IPA, fights the taste while the alcohol helps him feign delight in being at the bar. Both get comfortable, take off their jackets to reveal four arms splotched with tattoos. A portion of shoulder glossed with a detailed Batman peeks out from Moose's sleeve; it's one of the first tattoos Munkey inked onto another person when he started training to become a tattoo artist shortly after high school. At the time, he wanted to believe he gave Moose's skin a better personality, something to differentiate Moose from other Black guys he and their high school friends knew or knew of, but now he can imagine what the traditional Mexican men think when they stare at Moose: "Is he Black or one of us?"

"Freakin' excited to drink with you again, dude," Munkey says, grinning wide as Moose nods cautiously, sipping his terrible beer. "Feel like we haven't done this in, like, what? A year? Two?"

"My birthday," Moose says.

"Fuck yeah," Munkey says. "When you introduced me to Lucy."

This is how Munkey remembers meeting his soon to be ex-wife, Lucy. Moose, however, distinctly remembers being no such wingman. In a crowd that filled Moose's then-new apartment, Moose and Lucy stood in the corner and talked the night away as everyone else danced and drank. They'd met in a summer algebra class during college, striking up conversation because they were the only tattooed punks in the class. Despite their connection and comfort, they never dated. Any romantic feelings were hesitant and kept from one another for years. This particular birthday, however, the drinks and the new home and Moose's new year of life geared them both up to break the platonic monotony.

Munkey arrived late to the party, already drunk, staring holes into Lucy, which Moose noticed immediately. Within moments, Munkey wove through Moose's crowded apartment and slipped in next to a newly annoyed Moose, touching elbows as they both held solo cups like clichés. Munkey asked if he heard Moose and Lucy talking about music and began to give his two cents on Iron Maiden and Metallica, using Spanglish like a weapon. Oscillating between English and Spanish to Moose's monolingual frustration, Munkey complimented Lucy's laugh, her electric blue hair, her fresh tattoo of an Aztec calendar on her chest peeking out from her The Cure halter top. Several drinks later, after Munkey booted Moose out of the trio by switching the conversation completely to Spanish, Lucy and Munkey kissed.

Through Lucy, Moose later learned that she and Munkey went back to his place and had sex that neither found pleasant; Lucy felt guilty about sleeping with one of Moose's friends, a friend she'd found too machista for her liking before the alcohol, while Munkey simply struggled to perform. After that night, however, Moose saw them both infrequently, but Munkey and Lucy kept seeing each other, became serious within months, married in a year. Moose ignored the invite to their wedding.

*

"Did I make it weird with Moose?" Munkey asked El Paisa at Munkey and Lucy's wedding reception, both men completely drunk from the open bar. The two met in high school, and though Munkey had known Moose longer, he found himself gravitating toward El Paisa—his Mexican heritage, his style, his speech, his machismo, everything Munkey's own father wanted out of his son. El Paisa, also unlike Moose, ignored being biracial, rarely acknowledging his mother's Salvadorian blood so that his father's Mexican roots could help him blend in with the brand of manhood their hometown begged of their men. "Comer asada, joder mujers," El Paisa's father used to beat into him. "Sé un verdadero hombre. Cerotes no pueden enseñarte eso."

"Nah, foo," El Paisa said to Munkey. "You deserve a full-blooded Mexican hyna. Moose is barely half Latino. What was he gonna do with her? Sabes que, if he's mad, let him be mad. He can find some other mayate to wife."

*

In the hometown bar, *yo sé perder, quiero volver* echoes out of speakers and buzzed mouths, and Munkey is not ready to talk about either Lucy or El Paisa leaving him. He enjoys Moose's laughter too much; joy bursts from his lungs like it did in their kindergarten days. So much so, that they start talking about Batman like they're five again, still weird looking to the other kids in Southeast LA who took aim at Moose's high yellow skin, Munkey's jutting ears, and both of their curly hair. Regardless of the teasing, they both loved Batman, so they talked Batman for decades.

"I still hate the fight scenes," Munkey tells Moose after reminiscing about seeing *Batman Begins* in theaters in tenth grade. "The camera moved too fast. Couldn't see him hit nobody."

"They implied the fights," Moose says, trying to play along, trying to finish his IPA. "Movie was all about overcoming fears and traumas and using psychology over brawn and all that shit. You don't gotta be all macho all the time. Don't gotta use your fists for goddamn everything."

"Pinche 'implied' and 'traumas' and shit," Munkey says mockingly. "No wonder you're a professor. Always smarter than the rest of us."

Neither agreed on a whole lot in terms of their *specific* tastes. At first, they shared a love for aggressive music. Both frequented their hometown's local punk venues and backyard shows, both joined separate bands among the zeitgeist, gave themselves "punk" names they swore to never grow out of. But over time, "Blacky Moose" and "Dürty Munkey" cut adjectives, claiming brevity and nothing more, and their tastes diverged. Munkey worshiped heavy metal and all its brutality, while Moose leaned harder into punk's political messaging. Their first fights formed during lunch hours at school.

"Punk is weak," Munkey said in a sleeveless *Kill 'Em All* Metallica shirt.

"There's no substance in metal," Moose said in a do-it-yourself Bad Brains T-shirt.

"Punk is for white boys, foo."

"Metal is for meathead rapists."

Now, at the bar, no one fights. Both men laugh off the Batman disagreements; even Moose's smile starts to form without effort. Someone puts in some change to keep the corridos rolling. Munkey orders another IPA, but Moose requests something tastier and lighter. Before any remnants of the high school fights surface, before this reunion can be undone by the pasts neither man can let die, Munkey sticks a finger in Moose's sleeve and lifts it up to see the Batman. He asks Moose how the bat is holding up, admiring how his work continues to live firmly within Moose's skin. Moose rolls the rest of the sleeve up to reveal an angry caped crusader in a blueish cowl, blood cradling his knuckles, teeth gnashed as though biting through an animal's flesh. It's still Munkey's favorite work, and he's happy it will live on Moose's body past his own expiration.

"Still one of my favorite tattoos," Moose says with a fresh Gose. Munkey's eyebrows furrow at "one of," but when he tries to ask, what do you mean *one of*? all that comes out are slurred letters. Moose asks him to repeat what he said, but Munkey waves it off, afraid of losing this moment where he and Moose can share a beer without bitterness weighing on their shoulders. He's hopeful more beers will help Moose feel the right amount of sympathy when they inevitably bring up El Paisa's passing. Munkey withholds snark, withholds "You're *one of* my favorite friends, Blacky," because he is still not ready to talk about El Paisa; he is still trying to keep El Paisa beautiful.

*

Moose never got along with Munkey's best friend, especially in high school. Every time Moose heard *the slur* thrown at him, it usually came from El Paisa's mouth, a symptom of the false comfort of his knowing a single Black person: access to the word without repercussions. That is how high school boys became friends after all—emotional violence.

Their group thrived on insults—toward moms, distant fathers, clothes, mannerisms, dreams, toward their own culture, toward other people's cultures. Slurs and slurs and on and on and on because it was harder to be damaged by white people when they spent all their time destroying themselves. El Paisa often led the charge, verbalizing attacks to galvanize his machismo, to flaunt his American freedom of speech as though armor protecting from la migra. A model citizen by way of self-flagellation.

Despite El Paisa's love for America, he came to school dressed full chunti every single day—clothes so loud, others around him became faceless. Every day, the brown cowboy hat, the blue long-sleeve button down, the Wranglers, the snakeskin boots.

"Pinche paisa thug over here," Munkey would say in admiration. Moose never got it, but El Paisa's faceless friends fawned over El Paisa, his "realness," his proximity to a manhood learned by watching his Salvadorian mother collapse to his Mexican father's words and fists. Over time, El Paisa spat on his mother's flag, believing her blood too weak to survive the hometown. In the few occasions El Paisa owned his Salvadorian half, he called himself a mutt and laughed. El Paisa's faceless friends wanted his thick skin, his fragile solidarity, especially after seeing how El Paisa treated

Moose, whom he referred to as, at best, "my fellow mutt," and at worst, "the only mayate we like."

When El Paisa patted Moose on the back and said, "Oh, sorry Blacky. Don't know if the scars healed yet," everyone laughed. When El Paisa asked Moose if he and the charred black gristle underneath the cafeteria stove were relatives, everyone laughed. When El Paisa took some of the guys on a drunken joyride through a pitch-black park deep into a Saturday night and pondered, "We could accidentally run over Blacky and we'd never know," Moose heard that everyone laughed. Moose heard Munkey laughed the hardest.

"Hit us back," Munkey begged Moose, swearing he could learn to laugh with everyone.

Moose refused for most of high school until, after a particularly relentless lunch, he bolted for honors trigonometry as the others slowly made their way toward metal shop. The Mexican boys shunned Moose for walking so fast toward class, urging him to stay a little longer and talk more bullshit. Maybe even ditch.

"Come on," they pressured as Moose walked faster toward class. "Let's skip out for some burgers or something."

"Don't be lame, you gorilla-faced motherfucker," Munkey laughed.

All the guys "Oh'ed" as though a fight were ready to ignite. Moose stopped and turned toward El Paisa's faceless friends, all those Mexican boys, staring them down like a duel.

"I'm tryna get degrees, and not tryna to stand in front of Home Depots after we graduate like y'all are!"

The laughter became erupted lava, just as destructive. Pride carved into the Mexican boys like self-harm. El Paisa keeled over in tears, laughing harder than Moose or Munkey had ever heard. Moose walked away with a smirk as a chorus of "oh's" colored his footsteps, but he still could not laugh with them. The very next time Moose and El Paisa crossed paths, El Paisa put a brotherly hand on Moose's shoulders to say, "You got us good, Blacky. You got us good."

*

"I'm so sorry, man," Munkey says at the bar after Moose has finished telling a story about some students refusing to take him seriously for the sin of being a young, Black and brown professor with "all the cool tattoos."

"You deserve respect," Munkey slurs as another IPA empties into his gullet with a third on its way; Moose enjoys his Gose nice and slow. "You Black, you brown, you still young. Who gives a fuck, right? Fuck. I'm sorry. Shoulda never gave you that Batman tattoo, man. If your skin were cleaner, they'd respect you. But I fucked that up."

"What the fuck are you talking about?" Moose asks, amused and scared, slowly reverting to the regret of showing up to the bar. "I love this tattoo."

"Are you sure?" Munkey asks, clear. "Which tattoo do you love most, though?" he asks, less clearly. Moose asks for a repeat, but Munkey does not oblige. They try to finish talking about work, about Moose's tenure as a community college instructor, about Munkey finishing his apprenticeship at the local tattoo parlor, but the words are getting lost in the clouds of boozy breath. Moose looks at his beer, measuring how much he has left to drink before he can pay the tab and leave. After *Nos dejamos hace tiempo pero me llego el momento de perder* croons for what feels like a third time, Munkey croons himself.

"You don't deserve that shit, man. I'm sorry, I'm sorry, I'm sorry."

Moose does not ask what Munkey is sorry for, dreading it would have anything to do with El Paisa; afraid the vitriol he has for El Paisa would splash over Munkey. Moose downs the rest of his Gose and reaches for his wallet when Munkey grabs his arm.

"Foo, you're not leaving yet, right?" Munkey asks, smiling as tears curdle in his eyes. El Paisa is not here, he cannot be here.

Moose lets go of his wallet, asks Munkey to stop saying "sorry" and assures him that they are having a good time.

*

Moose would have preferred the "sorry" during their final high school lunch. Everyone signed yearbooks and talked about futures. Moose was college bound while everyone else had jobs lined up with various friends and relatives. El Paisa signed up for the Marines. His brother, proud, gifted him a sapphire-blue *balisong* knife for protection in case his gun ever failed him. El Paisa spent the lunch bragging about heading to boot camp directly after graduation, then proceeded to show off knife skills he learned from his brother.

The weapon is colloquially known as a "butterfly knife" because of its dual handles, which mimic a wingspan, and the fluttering that precedes the knife's opening and closing. An erudite twist of the wrist unleashes a blade sharpened to open skin; pirouetting handles are a spectacle to distract prey. El Paisa played with the knife for hours upon receiving it—later, it became meditation to pass time during tours. That last high school lunch, he flung the knife around effortlessly; everyone rapt by the blade comfortably under El Paisa's control. Eyes locked by beautiful violence, his friends waited for each trick, confident that El Paisa would pull them all off bloodlessly. El Paisa did not ruin a single twist, did not botch one toss, his hands clean of knicks, demonstrating how the knife's acrobatics were more graceful than a butterfly.

Despite white deans walking past their table during the exhibition, no one stopped El Paisa. With the school year ending, many faculty and staff decided that keeping the students from violence was no longer within their jurisdiction. The bell rang as Munkey was about to sign Moose's yearbook. Too spellbound by El Paisa to write anything substantial, Munkey wrote:

To BLACKY!!!
Yea the bell just rang
so take care.
—Munkey

After graduation, everyone went their separate ways for entire years until a New Year's Eve carne asada at Munkey's backyard. The timing aligned with Moose's return from college and El Paisa's return from the military. No one had changed much; Moose still wore punk clothes, Munkey still wore metal clothes, and El Paisa wore his cowboy hat over a shaved head. Other friends faceless as ever. Everyone stood around the fire pit as midnight approached. Alcohol flowed freely, and even Moose and El Paisa felt bold enough to trade pleasantries.

"How's my fellow mutt doin' these days?" El Paisa asked with a half-smirk, holding a half-empty beer in one hand, blue balisong in the other. "Didn't get pulled over on the way over here, did ya? Or did you remember to tell them you're also Costa Rican?"

"I'm still your only Black friend, aren't I?" Moose asked El Paisa, attempting to reciprocate the humor he never understood.

"All I need is one," El Paisa said, mindlessly flicking his balisong as he spoke, the blade dirtied with miniscule spots of dark red stained on the steel. The handle flew around in El Paisa's impatient clutch, a moth thirsty for fire. Someone said, "Tell us about how you saved your commander, foo." El Paisa smiled, regaling everyone with his version of events.

"Towelhead tried to merk our Sergeant," he said. "I caught the little bitch, gave her a bullet between the eyes. Simple as that."

Munkey, several tequila shots deep into the night, demanded everyone cheers to El Paisa's heroism. He slurred "Salut!" as everyone raised a glass. An unimpressed Moose kept his beer in his lap, and El Paisa looked down at his flying blade among friends yelling, "Viva El Paisa!" Munkey knew the full story, though, the one El Paisa kept in his chest. Upon returning to the United States for the first time since his initial deployment, El Paisa gave Munkey the details while sitting at the hometown bar, demanding Munkey tell no one. Munkey kept his promise, bending truths in his head until even he believed El Paisa was the hero he pictures now. Still, when his guard is down or his eyes are closed, Munkey sees El Paisa's balisong fail him.

Fellow soldiers patrolled a bombed building midday, and one marine caught a bullet to the face. The shooter was a middle-aged Iraqi man trying to get his family out of the area and out of sight of the marines. Spotted, the man, engulfed in fear, shot the marine. The shot only left a flesh wound in the marine's cheek that would heal over time and leave a "manly" scar. Their sergeant, less than a moment after the marine hit the ground, shot and killed the Iraqi.

Then a girl no older than ten—the man's daughter, they assumed—ambushed the soldiers. She surprised El Paisa, shoved him to the floor, and snatched his pistol and balisong. She aimed the pistol at the sergeant's head, but El Paisa regrouped fast enough to fire M4 rounds into the little girl. The force of the bullets spun her around into a violent ballet; her feet twirled on the floor, the balisong fluttering to the ground and contorting as if performing interpretive dance. Her eyes stayed open as she hit the ground, as though capturing the world one more time before death, as though trying to find butterflies she would never catch—ones not made from steel.

El Paisa's friends, and even El Paisa himself, never hear this version.

Yo se perder
Quiero Volver

Moose finished his beer despite the cheers, getting up to get a new bottle from the chest next to El Paisa, ignoring the count-down. The guys burst into cries of "¡Feliz Año Nuevo!" just as fireworks started shouting into the sky. One particular pop set off by a neighbor's roman candle exploded close to the backyard. El Paisa jumped out of his seat and readied his balisong, pointing the tip inches away from Moose's face. Everyone froze, then El Paisa laughed the knife away as the fire in the sky dispersed into smoke.

"Just thought you were tryna steal my wallet, mayate," El Paisa laughed.

Moose did not.

*

AAAAAHHHHHHHHH HA HA HA HAAAAAAAAAAAAAAAAAAA
The jukebox plays "Volver, Volver" again, and Munkey orders a fifth beer as Moose inches toward the end of his third. Munkey demands Moose take a shot with him, ordering two shots of mezcal before Moose can answer. Moose sees Munkey slowly leave his own body with every drop of beer, and with a cheers so erratic the mezcal flings out of the shot glass and onto Munkey's pants. He shoots what's left of the mezcal, orders another shot, shoots that one too. Moose pretends to shoot but puts the glass down when Munkey isn't looking.

"You, you gotta stay, man," Munkey begs before slamming Moose's rejected shot. "We're having a good time, good good time right now. I owe you, foo. So much. So fucking much. I met Lucy because of you. You gotta stay. Then she'll stay."

Moose wants to leave, no longer patient enough to ask Munkey again to translate his drunken slurs. As Moose motions toward an exit—empty glass, shuffling for a wallet, checking for belongings—Munkey again wraps an iron hand around Moose's arm. Munkey wants his friend, and he wants him here.

"You still play, Moose?" Munkey asks. Moose gives in, slides back into his seat. They try to have a conversation about music, about playing guitar with soul, but Munkey pivots to speed and weight.

"I still play metal, man," Munkey says. "Metal is fucking big. So heavy. Con huevos. None of that punk shit. No offense. I just can't stand that 'Bikini Kill' fuckin' 'girls to the front' bullshit or

76

whatever. Lucy loves that shit. I know you do, too, but I don't get it. Where's the brutality, man? Where's the guitar solos?"

Munkey plays an air guitar; he plays it fast. Moose's eyes wander to the tables full of empty glasses as patrons' drunk singing grows rowdier than before. The PA system does not stand a chance, and Munkey's sudden, "Pongan Mötley Crüe. Pinche 'Home Sweet Home'!" drowns in the noise. Munkey jams faster, his strumming hand colliding with the bar two or three times. He feels nothing but music no one else can hear.

"El Paisa told me I looked stupid when I play guitar," Munkey says, his gesticulations quelled with a sudden burst of sorrow, staring off into the distance as though looking for someone. Moose takes this opportunity to move Munkey's beer away from him, hoping the bartender will see the move and cut them off.

"Last time I saw him," Munkey says. "Some pinche TGI Friday's. Was me, El Paisa, and his hyna Mari. He loved her, fool. Full-blooded Mexicana. Loved her. But she, like, wasn't happy the whole time we were there. Fuckin' 'Every Rose Has Its Thorn' blasting on the speakers and she wasn't happy? Nah! So, I'm jammin' out and El Paisa's all like, 'Tch, foo, you look stupid,' like I was embarrassing them or some shit. Said he hated that country-ass bullshit, but I didn't give a fuck. So I kept jammin' out. If I stopped, I woulda saw how fuckin' unhappy Mari was, which would remind me how unhappy Lucy was. Plus, foo, Mari's eyes were dark as fuck. Like, she overdid it with the eyeshadow, especially her right eye. Shit was so big it almost colored over this fresh scab on the side of her forehead.

"Moose, I'm not fuckin' stupid. She was barely able to drink water without the glass shaking like a motherfucker. Every time El Paisa even turned her way, she flinched. But I don't wanna think about my friends like that. Because my friends are perfect and fuckin' beautiful. So, I kept jammin', hoped Mari would start to be happy, that her eyeshadow would go away if I just stopped looking. But El Paisa, every time, 'Foo, you look fuckin' stupid.' And I'm not stupid, I know I'm not, but I didn't know how to believe that. Lucy is tryna leave me, some shit about needing more or feeling tied down. I don't fuckin' know. But I came to El Paisa and Mari hoping their love would rub off on me and fix us. All El Paisa told me was, 'Lucy's just being a woman. She'll come around.' Said women are loyal so long as they are reminded. Said, 'Foo, if she's still disrespecting you, find yourself another hyna. She'll change her tune real quick.' Then we drank more, and I jammed out until the song ended."

*

Moose will see Lucy days after the bar to mediate against a divorce; a drunken favor for Munkey. Moose and Lucy will meet for pho in a different city to escape the stench of their teens. Moose in a car, Lucy from a bus. When they talk, Munkey is in neither of their mouths. He is back in their hometown, recovering, hoping Moose will bring Lucy back to him. But when Moose and Lucy sit across from each other by the window where the sun and passersby can see them clearly, they will continue laughing at the same jokes they'd told years ago. Lucy's blue hair will give way to undyed roots, but her hands will be lighter, almost weightless, as she motions them with frenetic joy conversing with Moose. Moose will wish he can hold the weight of her hands, but he stays quiet to make sure Lucy's words are uninterrupted, ebullient, and hers alone. Munkey cannot enter this conversation; he stands far from the window, cities away, petrified of the cuts that come from reaching through glass too violently.

"Honestly, fuck him," Lucy will say, telling Moose all about El Paisa's last few months on earth, truths Munkey would not spit out back at the bar. "Mari told me she came home to find El Paisa with another woman in their bed, still thrusting even after Mari called out in horror two or three times. Fucker didn't think anything was wrong. No matter what anyone tells you, he put his hands on her first. Wanted to beat his mother out of her. They struggled to the floor next to his pants. She saw El Paisa's butterfly knife sticking out of the pocket." Said the blue handle's wings looked like a sleeping bat; El Paisa's fists got angrier, his knuckles hungry to cave her bones as a lesson, so she woke up the bat to save her life. Grabbed the balisong, thrust the blade into El Paisa's abdomen, then his dick. "Several times. He let go. Mari escaped. Her wounds will heal, Moose. Gonna give her brand new skin.

"Munkey refuses to believe that's the story. Refuses to hear anything else about what happened. Never found out if there was a lawsuit or what happened to the remains of that asshole's junk. But Munkey cried when he found out El Paisa returned to tour after being medically cleared—whatever that meant. Cried harder when the mortar took him. Blamed El Paisa's injuries, said they made it harder for him to run. Honestly, I think he was just stupid enough to point the mortar straight up into the air, probably thought it wouldn't come back down because he was invincible, or some machista bullshit. Regardless, we went to the funeral. Munkey begged me to go with him, even after I said I wanted a divorce. El Paisa's mom cried when soldiers draped an American flag over his casket. She's his only living parent—his dad's heart stopped working after El Paisa's first tour—so they flew a Mexican *and* Salvadorian flag during the ceremony; I watched the wind blow the blue and white coat of arms over the eagle with a snake in its mouth."

Lucy will finish telling this story. Lucy will not return to Munkey. Lucy will laugh and let Moose laugh with her, as though no one has died, because Lucy is tired of men laughing, tired of their tears superseding hers. She's tired, and will sleep like a bat who saved a life.

*

"Everyone leaves," Munkey says through ruptured, intoxicated jargon, the bartender having just told him he's done for the night.

"You left. Then El Paisa. Now Lucy's tryna split. I can't let her go. I'm her man. She gotta have her man. She gotta come back. You came back, Moose. Fuck. But El Paisa. Mari ain't got her man. El Paisa can't come back."

Moose cannot understand any of it, attempts to get ahold of Munkey so they can leave the bar together, says he'll walk him to the curb to catch a rideshare. Munkey's limbs hang on marionette strings, and now he sees two Mooses; one brown, one Black. Munkey grabs one shoulder like a brother, but his other hand stays inert on the bar for a few moments. Still, there is enough power to reel Moose in for a hug. Munkey grips Moose's body like an iron maiden, Munkey's body shakes from balance escaping his legs. Moose's arms are trapped at his sides, unable to reciprocate a hug even if he wanted to.

"He ain't got no dick," Munkey cries with his first formed words in several minutes. "A man gotta have his dick. Now he's dead."

The wails draw the bar's attention once again as Vicente Fernández no longer croons. Munkey's tears roll down the back of Moose's jacket; both their eyes are closed, from pain, from embarrassment. Moose cannot reach his wallet. Moose cannot lace his hands around Munkey. Moose cannot ignore the chatter competing with Munkey's drunken cries, an errant and barely whispered, "Pinche negrito y maricón," hurled their direction. Moose cannot get the picture of El Paisa out of his head; eunuched, disintegrated, his tongue torn apart by warfare—a tongue that lashed Moose's back for years, a tongue that lassoed a kindergarten Munkey away from a young Moose, a tongue that laughed and laughed. Now Moose is laughing. His laughter trounces Munkey's crying, eclipsing all the chatter in the bar. Now all eyes whelm the two. Munkey's clasp loosens from Moose's convulsing shoulders, lets go in anger. The laughter does not stop.

"Stop laughing," Munkey yells. "It's not funny!"

With a backfired shove, Munkey loses his balance and crashes to the floor along with a couple of empty beer glasses. Munkey's strumming hand grips pieces of broken glass, but he does not feel a thing. Other men in the bar get up to do nothing but watch the commotion—even Moose refuses to offer a hand to Munkey. On the floor, Munkey stares at his sliced palm, the blood drips like drool. He looks up to see four Mooses: a Black, a brown, a punk, a child.

"Ayúdame, Blacky," Munkey asks Moose, who stands above him, his violent laughter tempered to light chuckles. "Talk to my wife, yeah? Ask Lucy to stay with me? I'll get our tab. You won't owe me anything."

"I already know that," Moose says. "I'm going home, so take care."

The four bodies vanish from Munkey's view, but men still crowd around the glass. The broken pieces are stained-glass prayers to Munkey's younger self, slices that will scab one day and become a reminder, a eulogy. For now, not even Chente's voice consoles him as Munkey peels shards of glass from his hand like fleas from fur.

Heredia Becomes America

rascacielos son árboles con ventanas.

lo siento. *papi says to say, "skyscrapers," because that is what we are supposed to call them now.*

people inside the trees see us fly. we fly to them—papi says "asi es como aceptan."

hummingbirds sing inside the crown.

el sol de ellos es mio tambien.

i want to rest on their boughs to watch the sun the way they do, un feliz perezoso asleep in the security of skyscrapers heredia could not grow.

The red-eyed tree frog lives in the rainforests of Costa Rica. Eyes glow the color of blood to ward off hunters, to make them believe frogs can eat lions whole. It climbs branches with suction-cup toes and can reach the tops of leaves with ease. Its skin blends into these leaves to hide from predator teeth, to become foliage, to pretend to be Earth.

The red-eyed tree frog only looks for a partner in the rain. Gray clouds ward off heat. Liquid helps to slip out of claws. When red-eyed tree frogs decide to mate, they wait until nightfall. They wait for stars to be the only eyes that stare back into the red—the non-violence is an aphrodisiac. When they are good and ready, they lay eggs on the underside of leaves, hanging above the safety net of water. Earth is a midwife holding these children with its green hands.

Mamá is forty-two, and she hates dogs. "We had a German shepherd for six years before you were born," she tells me. "His name was Ace. Big, loud, he scared the neighbors. White people on the block looked at Ace with fear, then at us with disappointment. He left holes in the grass, and bite marks carved into our Sarchi chairs. I didn't want to go outside when he was awake.

"But your grandparents loved Ace. Papi said every good American family had perritos. *He* said white people looked at us with jealousy, that they wished their dogs were as big as ours. Wished their dog could hop a six-foot gate in a single jump to scare off thieves. *He* said the gringos should feel lucky Ace didn't jump over and eat them.

"Over time, he tore up the house and had more frequent accidents. Pieces of our furniture scattered everywhere; Ace's gums bled with Papi's precious grass. We got the wrong kind of attention from the gringos. The day we gave him away everyone cried except me."

Mamá tells me this story every time I even hint at wanting a pet. I tell Mamá I want a Jack Russell terrier. I go to bookstores and libraries to read up on taking care of them, give Mamá an encyclopedic rundown of what the care entails. She refuses because they pee on things.

"That's what perritos do," she says. "Pee on things."

Mamá hates any mess she doesn't know how to immediately clean up, especially made by babies and dogs: neither can speak to Mamá the way she knows how to speak. Accidents happen, then she's forced to clean up after a creature who had no chance of telling her what they truly wanted. "At least babies grow up and learn how to speak," she says. "Animals don't talk. They don't have language. They just bark. So violent."

"I still don't know Spanish," I remind her. "Does it make me an annoying baby when you're talking to grandma and I don't know what you're saying?"

Mamá never taught me Spanish, often blaming Pops. "He never learned Spanish either, so he didn't want *us* talking shit behind his back," she says. Sometimes, she retells her story of coming to America in the third grade, then stops to say, "I just wanted you to avoid some stuff I went through coming here." I am not only the one kid in school who doesn't know Spanish, I am also the only kid whose family doesn't have a dog.

Instead of a Jack Russell terrier, I am gifted a turtle. His name, at first, was Squirtle. Then I turn thirteen and his name becomes Mortimer. My parents cannot stand the smell of his tank. I say, "I'll clean it in a second," too often. Pops cleans it for me when my "second" takes too long. Eventually, Pops stops waiting for me. I start to forget how to take care of Mortimer, how to clean his tank, never learn what kind of food he likes best. Soon, he stops being Mortimer and becomes "my turtle," then "the turtle." Within the year, Pops gets fed up. One night, he takes the tank out on to the street and leaves it by the curb where neighbors leave box springs and used furniture. I spend the night crying, losing a pet I barely touched. The room's darkness deepens without the turtle's tank light that once sat comfortably at my bedroom door. Then, like a switch, I stop crying. Tears dry on my cheek, then I am just tired.

I still want a Jack Russell terrier. I know I could love it despite the pee. I know I could hear beyond the panting and the barks. But I can never convince Mamá, who once tried to pet a dog at a friend's birthday party until its teeth ate through the arm of her windbreaker.

This land is ___ land, this land is my land

(¿dónde está el baño? ¿dónde está el baño? ¿dónde está el baño?)

from California to ___ ___ Yo(u)r_ Island

(¿where está el baño? where está el baño?)

From the _____ forest, to the ____ ____ waters

(where es el baño? where es de baño?)

This land was made for ___ ___ me

(¿where is ___ bathroom? ¿por favor?)

89

Yellow-bellied sea snakes absorb a third of their oxygen from seawater. They are marvelously slim, and they hunt for food in aquatic life. Normally, yellow is only prominent on a native snake's belly, hidden from view of red-eyed predators as it slithers along surfaces. Its back, the most prominently seen feature of the snake, is a distinct brown that leaves the snake invisible as it moves. Some yellow-bellied sea snakes in Costa Rica, however, are completely yellow. They abandon the brown all together to remain seen within the sea. For food, the yellow-bellied sea snake can eat several frog eggs from under a leaf in just one bite.

Mamá is nineteen, and the Virgen de Guadalupe stares at her uterus. The Planned Parenthood is infested with picket signs. Nonetheless, Mamá knows she can't have a baby right now. Pops holds his hands over her ears, and the vitriol becomes a low hum.

Pops just turned eighteen and knows his Black skin makes the white protestors hate him, too. They both know race mixing frightens her parents just as much as these protestors, makes them cry like the white Jesus superglued to cardboard next to the clinic's door, and would disappoint them like the day they met Pops for the first time.

"¿Él es negro?"

"Yes! So? I love him!"

Neither of my parents want to disappoint the elders, and they rush inside the building. Pops holds Mamá as the protestors' shouts dissolve into the clinic. When the red comes out of her, it's as if no one is there. She swallows her screams with her thighs warmed by blood she was not ready to know. Pops protectively cups Mamá's ears on the way out, but the sound is already gone. The protestors' howls sound as if caught underwater. The Virgin in her green shawl watches over Mamá without judgement.

Mamá is thirty-nine.
I ask her politely for a sibling.
Brother.
Sister.
Someone else to call her "mother."
I wait for her answer, confused by her tears.

¡PINCHE PERRA MALA!

¡PERRA MALA!

¡STUPIDA!

¡PUTA!

¡PENDEJA!

¡STUPIDA!

mi cama está llena de tierra, pero está bien.

they tell me cucarachas walk on my arms when i sleep, but i do not feel them.

papi says we do not need outhouses in América, that we can stay inside when storms are too loud for the bathroom.

we leave soon, but for now the rain stains the outhouse with water, y mi pijamas está empapas—they cling to my body like dirt that will not wash off my skin.

i wonder if América lets bugs sleep without us?

if toilets can be left inside while everything stays dry.

outside, i see heredia's hills become light; orange streetlights are haloes, se convierten en estrellas bajo la lluvia.

The northern cat-eyed snake, scientifically known as *Leptodeira septentrionalis*, colloquially known as, "Oh, shit! What is that?!" has a bite that only affects a human's pain receptors as much as a bee sting, since its venom is too mild to stun. No matter, when the northern cat-eyed snake is hungry and cannot find an adult red-eyed tree frog, tadpoles make an exquisite alternate meal.

Mamá is thirty and celebrates her birthday in the hospital. I have only been alive for one month, but my lungs have already failed. It started with food unable to enter my stomach, but the wheezing frightened her the most. To this day, she doesn't remember the disease's name, but maybe that's the way to kill the poison of memory.

She watches incubators spread past the viewing window like a minefield. I am a scorched shell. Nurses ask if she needs coffee, or water, or food. Mamá fights to not say, "I want air in my baby's lungs. Can you get me that?" Instead, "No, thank you," with barren breasts, eyes locked on her suffocating bomb.

She refuses to admit she never wanted children, never wanted a child to know how painful it is to fight to live. America was meant to let us live without ailment. Her newborn is already dying. Mamá prays I will find language to say, "I am OK now."

The disease will let me live, and my stomach will have a deep scar on the right side of my abdomen. Mamá looks at the wound as a reminder of the battles she wanted me to avoid, whose fists still found my bones. Soon after I am diffused, Mamá decides against a second child. Her tubes are tied. She argues with Pops, who hoped for me to have siblings. This hope lasts years, a lifetime. But Mamá doesn't fear an umbilical cord around her baby's neck anymore. Rosary beads no longer fissure her palms. Thirty years later, the scar still brands me like a prison tattoo—like any good child of an old-fashioned Latina, I keep my shirt on around her to hide the ink, to keep her thinking my skin is pure.

the american kids laugh without me.
jajajas.
my mouth is closed.
i cannot make jello sound like yellow the way they want it.
i cannot open my mouth fast enough to show them my tongue
is the same colors as theirs.
their flag—the whites, the reds, the blues, "son mios tambien!"
pero, como se dice "where is the bathroom" en ingles?
no one will tell me.
does it translate to, "please stop threatening my auburn hair.
please stop telling me my tiara is rusted.
please let me go to the bathroom because i thought i escaped
the pain of storms that eat my roof like a predator.
if i mutate my words into yours, make sure my babies do not
make the mistake of sharing my language, will you let us go?
if i turn my hair jello, will you stop laughing?"
i do not know how to talk to teacher, now my feet drown in
pee—
teacher thinks that's just what i do.
he confiscated my tongue when i couldn't say his words.
a b cs erase ah beh cehs
my nose is wet with shame rubbed into pee stains.
now i see fangs instead of hummingbirds—they swim in the
jello around my ankles.
they hiss like bombs that take skyscrapers away from the eyes
of airplanes.

Years ago, for six days, I cared for a terrier mix. He is a puppy and not house trained. I live alone and work nonstop at multiple colleges to try and make ends meet. The terrier never listens, never learns, pees everywhere. On the third day, I try to pick him up to stop him from biting another piece of furniture, but he slides through my grip and smacks the linoleum like a meteorite. I hold his warm body, begging his fur for forgiveness. On the sixth day, I give him to a new family, relieved he is no longer in danger of being loved by me.

Mamá is sixty, and I am thirty. Mamá never learned that the red-eyed tree frog's tadpoles—native to her motherland—can survive without permission. They'll walk one day, proving they never knew what teeth felt like on their newborn skin. Red-eyed tree frogs' eventual suction-cupped limbs keep them clinging to Earth. Mamá should watch them hop in the rain to find safety in the cleansing water. Maybe then, she'll believe it when they learn to scale skyscrapers; they'll make homes high in the branches where no fangs can reach their legs, where their eyes adapt to scare predators the way their mother's eyes kept them safe from yellowed bellies.

"How come you never moved back to Costa Rica?" I ask her when I come over for a quick breakfast. We reminisce about visiting family in Costa Rica; I think about how free she looked speaking only Spanish to her loved ones, how dry she stayed basking under the Tico sun.

Mamá doesn't answer my question. Instead, she pulls up a picture on her phone of herself in the third grade. An old photo recently found among albums collecting dust in the back of a closet. Here, she had been away from Costa Rica only days. Here, she didn't know the other kids were afraid of roaches. She has dyed her hair blonde since the '80s, but here her hair is a lifegiving shade of tree bark; a Tica's crown whose auburn radiance shines.

"My nose was so big here, huh?!" she asks, trying to laugh. "The kids used to make fun of that, too. Said it looked like a dog's nose."

"No," I say. "Your nose is a fine nose."

It is a perfect nose. She stands in the photo, soaked in a luminous morning glow. Here, her posture sings the future. Here, trees surround her like a cornucopia exhaling a ripe fruit of the womb.

Here, she smiles despite America's venom, a smile that protects her tongue from the snakes. Here, she knows no English, but she is an American child who survives.

... Said the Dandelions

Overture

Scene

South Gate, CA.
Sometime in the late 1990s and throughout the 2000s.

The Player:
- THE CHILD

(Trust is taught to be a myth in South Gate.)

(All doors in the city are locked at night out of necessity. The most underprivileged houses must wear gates surrounding the yard, or bars fitted over windows like a warm sweater. Backyards are not where grass grows long for children to break their falls playing tag, but a stage illuminated by spotlights poured out by police helicopters; the actors are runners climbing fences and brick trying to escape the light, trying to find a backdoor without a lock so they can bust in and hide.

Look—the city devoid of whites. They flew away after the '70s, took the wealth with them, sawed off some of the gravel from South Gate so that the junk cars left over for the brown folk could be further beaten up by the ground. Whites flew away like dandelion seeds caught in the wind. People are in awe of the seeds as the stems freeze naked.

Here is a very small house. Adequately sized for an only child of a brown mother and a Black father. The house is rented—did you think it was owned? Don't be silly. Mountains of debt and bills kept the parents from even imagining home ownership. The living room and dining room are conjoined, the other side of the dining table blocked off due to lack of room. The stove is broken, and the heater does little else than stub toes.

See the window in the back of the child's bedroom, attached to a door leading to the backyard. A dresser blocks the door per the parent's request. The window is still visible, though a grate skewed the view to the backyard, can potentially skewer a robber's hand from reaching inside the home. On hot days, the window opens with grate bent at an angle to place a fan on top of it. It works fine until the child searches for a missing item on the floor; the rusted grate impales the top of the child's head. Palm painted in blood after putting pressure on the wound.)

THE CHILD
(Toward the audience. South Gate background dimmed to illuminate the aura of the child. He coddles his wound like a child of his own, hoping to raise a scab into a healthy scar.)

So much of life is spent proving you exist when all you've known of safety and comfort are locked doors. I've learned to find visibility through suffering. Though no one taught me where the suffering is supposed to go. Does it float away to evaporate into the air, or does it become hail and hurt everyone?

(The Child fades back into South Gate, now illuminated like a brush fire. The landscape is caked in weeds, little tombstones of forgotten grass.)

THE CHILD
(Offstage)
Oh, how I wish for the privilege of escape. To fly away like dandelions. I don't like it here. Take me to where this wound is no longer a wound. Please.

An Opera

SCENE:

Echo Park, CA.
Sometime in the mid-2010s.

The Players:

- COSTA RICAN, THE HALF BLACK
- MEXICAN WHO SAYS N███A
- CUBAN WITH PONTIAC
- GLORIA ANZALDÚA
- ARIANA BROWN
- FRANTZ FANON
- AYISHAT AKANBI
- DR. ALAN PELAEZ LOPEZ
- DANDELIONS [NAMES REDACTED. ETHNICITY WITHHELD]

(Dandelions are weeds with trust funds; their fragile white heads understood to be true beauty. They sprout throughout the Los Angeles area where oasis springs are pools of IPA, where The Echo oozes reverb of hipster guitars.

Dandelions want to be the ally to the marginalized. They want to live on the frontlines of violence and be louder than police bullets. Their voices are skeleton keys to unlock handcuffs fastened over profiled wrists. They think they want to understand the language of the other.

There is an apartment at the top of a hill. Party music spills into LA air through a window opened to appease musty guests. Inside, dozens of wallflowers with dandelion heads line the couches. They are under the impression that this is a party for the rejected—designated outsiders in the manner '90s sitcoms taught adolescents. A party for white kids whose glasses were too large, GPAs too high, face caked in pus, who were one removed scrunchie away from perfection; ignoring how they are the desired demographic.

The twenty-somethings play Super Smash Bros. Across tabletops, in case of boredom, board games sit with top-shelf tequila and Gentleman Jack. Among the white kids, three brown dots scatter like stars—each a different shade of brown, each knows the ground beneath Echo Park buried people like them. Each brown dot once lived in South Gate, but have moved on to greener pastures—as their mothers and abuelas begged them to do. When the three brown dots talk, they talk across the living room about crimes for which they freely plead guilty.

Costa Rican, the half Black sips a rum and coke from a red cup. Speaks to Mexican who says n█a, blacking out this friend's name to find solace in their conversation. Watch all their words, watch Cuban with Pontiac attentive to his skin folk as these three brown dots work together to understand the words that damage them. Watch Dandelions refuse to point their fragile heads toward all the words that hurt so many, all the words they've sowed themselves.)

COSTA RICAN, THE HALF BLACK

Mamá screamed, "Ejole gran puta idiota de chinito!" when we were almost sideswiped on a freeway. Didn't even see the driver. She just assumed.

(beat)

Really, Mamá called every Asian "chinitos." All of them. Chinamen. It's fucking annoying. Mamá laughs at the name, "Nguyen," because it sounds funny to her, yet she gets mad when people can't pronounce her own name. It's not like they'd confuse her for Latina since her skin is white as snow.

(beat)

She came to America when she was eight, then was immediately bullied because her language made no sense to the white kids. What'd she do? Learn the colonizer language to fit in. Got some of that sweet oppressor power to protect herself.

(beat)

But who am I to tell her that? She still slept with cockroaches and shat in holes in the dirt behind her shack growing up in Costa Rica. Fucking sucks. So, to not flaunt my degrees as though her own journey was a failure, best I can do to correct her is to say, "Mom, that's racist," when she uses "chinito." But she will just say, "Oh, is it? Damn, sorry."

(beat)

I'll give her this: Mamá cried for her Chinese watch repair woman. Passed away from a sudden stroke. The woman had a name, but *I* never learned it.

(beat)

Mamá remembered her. Said they never had a true conversation, but the wordlessness brought them together—no weight of expectation for understanding when we rely on actions. That's how she saw it, anyway. Mamá still speaks fondly, to this day, of the sweet Chinese woman named _____, who was actually Chinese—Mamá took the time to learn the woman's background.

(beat)

How proud I *should* be.

(The Dandelions can't find their mouths, can't vouch for the pride in admitting fault. No. They keep playing games and drinking to forget their own troubles, drown out three brown dots having their moments and trying to come to Jesus. All that good shit.)

GLORIA ANZALDÚA

The answer to the problem between the white race and the

colored, between males and females, lies in healing the split that originates in the very foundation of our lives, our culture, our languages, our thoughts. A massive uprooting of dualistic thinking in the individual and collective consciousness is the beginning of a long struggle, but one that could, in our best hopes, bring us to the end of rape, of violence, of war.

COSTA RICAN, THE HALF BLACK

Wishful thinking, bruh. I mean, I'm no angel, right? My Cambodian friend at work and I make fun of white people all the time. You know . . . because we can. We make fun of how racist some can be. Both purposefully and accidentally.

(Listen for Dandelions' laughter and nods. See the sweat. See the fear. Relief in interpreting "My Cambodian friend . . . " as permission for Dandelions to wear "My Black friend . . . " as shields.)

Then we'll make jokes about each other's cultures as if we know what it means to live in them. He'll make fried chicken jokes or elote jokes. I'll counter with, "Oh yeah! . . . well . . . Pol Pot!" He'll laugh, but almost out of some sense of self-hatred.

(Pol Pot listens in on the conversation among the wallflowers, but says nothing. Cambodian Prime Minister from 1975-1979, he feasts off the few who regard him as a champion of socialism and Cambodian sovereignty. Most keep him cornered as the dictator directly responsible for the Cambodian genocide during his rule. Listen to his sins as Dead Kennedy's "Holiday in Cambodia" play over the party speakers, a song lambasting the white liberals' search for culture within the suffering of marginalized groups—the white liberal who will wag a finger at fiends like Pol Pot without actually saving a Cambodian life.

Listen to the original recording: there are the lines, "play ethnicky jazz to parade your snazz on your five-grand stereo / bragging that you know how the niggers feel cold and the slums got so much soul." *Dandelions feel seen in this line but refuse to acknowledge such proximities to the slur. Instead, they condemn singer Jello Biafra's usage of the slur even if coated in irony, then they look at Costa Rican, the half Black for approval, then wait. Somewhere, Jello Biafra sings the song with "Blacks" in place of the offending slur, stripping the song of its honesty.)*

He legit hates the Chinese! Says they make Cambodians feel lower class. Says they look at Cambodians as dirty the way Mexicans see Central Americans. Says his other Cambodian friends just pretend they are Chinese to feel empowered and invisible from white pressures.

(Dandelions continue to hear, though it is unknown whether they are listening.)

It's all learned, right? Our parents tell us to look for violence in the eyes of people that don't look like us. When the whites refuse to make eye contact with us, they force us to search for violence elsewhere, inward, towards brothers and sisters.

(Dandelions refuse the shame but look down anyway. Their roots spread without their notice, but they don't stop it.)

Are we bad people? Are our parents bad people??

(Sweat of the Dandelions is dew.)

(Cuban with Pontiac is smiling with his fourth IPA half emptied, a blue cardigan haggled from an H&M sculpted over his body, long strands of auburn washed over his shoulders. While he indulges in white spoils, his tongue still knows Cuba: the tastes of Havana

without American spices, the remnants of torn Che Guevara propa-
ganda between his fingernails—how Mexican who says n███a
praises Che's revolutionary charisma as a benchmark for Latinx
freedom, how Cuban with Pontiac only hears the death throes of
Cuban ancestors in his voice.)

CUBAN WITH PONTIAC

Nah, man! We're not the bad guys. We can't be the bad guys.
But, I totally know what ya mean! My mom once told me this
joke when abuela gave me her hand-me-down car: the run-down
red number that's been through at least three owners in our
family alone. She goes, "You know what 'Pontiac' stands for,
right?"

(Nervous laughter spills from Cuban with Pontiac. Dandelions
stay glued to games. Furrow brows in nervous anticipation. Keys
to the current year's model car clung to their pockets. "Please
don't say the n-word," the hive mind prays. "We won't know how
to react with him around," they think, staring directly at Costa
Rican, the half Black.)

POOR OLD NIGGER THINKS IT'S A CADILLAC!

(Hold for applause. Hold for laughter. When neither arrive, watch
Dandelions convulse, seeds finally fly from their heads from the
mild wind. Nonetheless, their white crowns hold together. Costa
Rican, the half Black, however, fumes. Did not need to hear the
punchline because he knew the punchline already. Has lived being
a punchline too long to stand for what Cuban with Pontiac's mom
thinks is okay to say. Costa Rican, the half Black tries to black out
the joke, but it is too late. Cuban with Pontiac tries to explain.
We all carry on.)

I said, "Mom! You can't say that! But, you CAN say that, but

you can't say THAT! But, you can say THAT, but tact woman!
TACT, TACt, TAct, Tact, tact, tact, tact, tact, tact, tact, tact, tact, tact,
tact, tact, ~, tact, ~!
*(Now Mexican who says n███a. Che stands triumphant, silk-
screened on Mexican who says n███a's shirt. Gel slicks his hair
back like reins slowing a horse, and his smile also refuses to die.
In his red cup is a second Paloma, a favorite among his family—
stereotypes be damned. His jeans will be loose, and his skin is
golden despite Dandelions seeing rust. Mexican who says n███a's
vocabulary is molded by South Central, his influx of Black friends
doses him with a placebo of unity.)*

MEXICAN WHO SAYS N███A

It's not racist. It's a joke, right? I mean I have Asian friends,
Black friends.

(Points to Costa Rican, the half Black.)

I have grown up using, "n███a" like, "my n███a," like, "hey,
n███a how is the family. You look healthy. You look happy."

COSTA RICAN, THE HALF BLACK

Please stop using that word. Knowing a minimum-required-
amount of Black people doesn't give you the "n-word pass" bro.

MEXICAN WHO SAYS N███A

If we delete a word, toxins stay. Snakes can be defanged without
decapitation.

*(Briefly, watch Mexican who says n███a walk into a bar on a date.
After too many Palomas, he sees a Black man looking directly at
the two. The discomfort is palpable, and exit strategies learned in
South Central take over his body. He becomes Mexican who ways
n███er, like "you n███er." Soon, the letters escape confinement,*

and he says, "Hey, what are you looking at nigger? Don't stare at me like that," so that the Black man can feel the full poison of Mexican who says n███er's mouth. While his date will plead that he simply had too much to drink, several Black bouncers escort him outside. They take him to the alley where lights are extinguished, and they feed him bruises in hope to extract the word like teeth.

Do these fists teach when conversations fail? When synthesis actually pulls apart the body due to the comfort of a tongue sampling cultures, does that reinforce white supremacy when the hope was to dismantle? Can't the Dandelions speak to this?)

COSTA RICAN, THE HALF BLACK

Let me say this first—my grandma went to a priest when she found out Mamá was about to marry a Black man. My grandma always said that being Costa Rican means not wanting any trouble, but she forgets that her daughter faced more pushback from whites than Blacks when they first arrived in America. Trouble will always find us, but being together, this unity Mamá and Pops wanted to create, is what adds to the peace my grandma prays for. We can't have unlocked doors if we keep taking from each other. Watch, the second she stops being so anti-Black, she'll learn that she can have open doors without fear of a storm tearing down her home. Still, in her confessions, she tells the priest that her daughter is in danger. Priest basically just tells her, "Having fear is sin." Despite that, I can tell my grandma feels Mamá betrayed the ancestors.

GLORIA ANZALDUA

En boca cerrada no entran moscas.

(beat)

I remember one of the sins I'd recite to the priest in the confession box the few times I went to confession: talking back to my mother, hablar pa'tras, repelar. Hocicona, repelona, chismosa, having a big mouth, questioning, carrying tales are all signs of being malcriada.

ARIANA BROWN

Let me be clear. Spanish was given to my people
at the end of a sword, forced in our throats gory,
sharpened under the colonizer's constant eye.
Each rolled r is a red wet fingerprint pointing me back
to this. Spanish is not my native tongue. English isn't either.
The languages I speak are bursting with blood,
but they are all I have.

(Three brown dots cower at the thought of dislodging their mother tongue, but know—deep down—it could heal many things. How do you say "evolve" when ancestors hear "disrepair"? Sins can be snuffed by forgiveness, but when they are spoken out loud, they can maliciously deafen. Watch Dandelions thrive on the silences; make three brown dots believe their mouths bring violence when all they want is a world where their elders can live without fear.)

CUBAN WITH PONTIAC

Hey! Speaking of fear, remember that time youuuuuuuuuuuuuuuuu

(finger firmly planted in Costa Rican, the half Black's face.)

were, like, about to cancel your flight when you found out you were sitting next to an "A-RAB"?! Your words, not mine, dude! Like the time your family went to the airport a year or two after 9/11 and your cousin screamed, "HABIBS!!" when she saw a few Sikh men walking through the terminals, minding their own business.

(hold for laughter)

(While you wait, open this time capsule: not long after the Sikh men were villainized, three brown dots found representation in comedy, namely Carlos Mencia. His 2006 special, No Strings Attached, focused on levying racial stereotypes for laughs. Listen to the roar of laughter when Mencia details attacking an Arab. In the bit, he refers to them as "a la las." In the front row, a bald white man cheers loudest at the thought of executing an Arab; his arms flail in celebration, two devil horns formed in his risen fists.

In Costa Rican, the half Black's high school, a classmate repeats one of Mencia's jokes, specifically saying, "Don't worry teacher. I'm brown, but I'm not an 'a la la.'" Teacher gets mad. Teacher demands the student never use that phrase again. Teacher is Mexican, but would relinquish his patriotism if it meant his Arab peers could retain their humanity.)

Then you befriended the dude! 'member? You 'member! Hung out all the time. Consider him your brother. You even said like, "Man, Islam gets a bad rap! I'd totally convert to Islam once this lapsed Catholicism runs its course." Bruh, *you* couldn't even tell if you meant any of it. Like, you couldn't tell if you were being nice, or maybe the guilt of harboring the post-9/11 fears for so long terrified you because—despite being what you called, "a double minority"—this was white supremacy: scapegoating to prove you are not the problem. Then you totally don't own up to that past; you get too invested in being an ally to try *and fail* to erase your own sins. Allies are s'possedta frickin' help people, not alienate, not become invasive, not flaunt how 'woke' you've become while pretending you have no expectation of rewards, dude. It's totally a white thing to vacation in other people's cultures to build armor against accusations of racism, no matter how much you disguise it as tryna find an objective moral high ground. Like, do you get mad at your mom for the Asian stuff because you truly feel for Asians, or do you fear association with your problematic-ass parent will make you look bad? Who are you tryna impress?

(Hold for applause. The Dandelions pray their seeds will blow away in the ovation, but the whiteness stays. Carry on)

FRANTZ FANON

All forms of exploitation resemble one another. They all seek the source of their necessity in some edict of a Biblical nature. All forms of exploitation are identical because all of them are applied against the same "object": man.

(Beat. Dandelions continue to pray.)

I am enraged, I am bled white by an appalling battle, I am deprived of the possibility of being a man. I can't disassociate myself from the future that is proposed for my brother. Every one of my acts commits me as a man. Every one of my silences, every one of my cowardices reveals me as a man.

AYISHAT AKANBI

We have to make mistakes. Life is trial and error. Awareness is understanding how much you don't know. A lot of my beliefs and ideas are constantly being shattered, and I really welcome it. I don't know about an "objective" truth, but at least if you're someone seeking a deeper understanding, you welcome being wrong. It's a pleasure to be wrong because when you are wrong you are closer to being right. Maybe the first sign of knowing anything is knowing you know nothing at all.

(Dandelion heads sprawl to create silent outlines of the dots' feet. Three brown dots are surrounded by the weeds they are forced to call beauty; they waft in the winds of anonymity.)

Maybe our fear of using words will go away, too. In time, of course, if it even needs to. I mean, you and I have been friends for over a decade and I'm pretty cool with your dad, but I would never say *that* word!

(Flash forward. Birthday karaoke, Cuban with Pontiac turns twenty-nine. He has too much sake before singing/rapping along to Childish Gambino's "Bonfire" with some other brown friends and Dandelions. They drunkenly recite, "Gambino is a call girl / fuck you / pay me / brand new whip for these niggas like slavery," and Cuban with Pontiac screams the n-word with the soft 'A' as though his own ankles were freed of chains for the first time. Costa Rican, the half Black is in the audience for this, though he does not tell Cuban with Pontiac about the knots in his stomach every time Cuban said the word, especially not in front of the cheering Dandelions—NAMES STILL REDACTED. ETHNICITY STILL WITHHELD. Instead, Costa Rican, the half Black says, "Happy birthday. I love you. Good night." Leaves early, never brings it up again.

Flash forward has ended, so return to Echo Park. Pollen of the Dandelions has not yet turned the dots red from allergy. Costa Rican, the half Black reminisces but still struggles when he even thinks of "the n-word.")

COSTA RICAN, THE HALF BLACK

It's a frightening world when words are frightening. But please: "Black friend" is no excuse for "n█████er." Especially when you're brown. You should know better, bro. You, your moms, my moms. ~~We~~ You should all know better.

DR. ALAN PELAEZ LOPEZ

This wounding of Latinidad via anti-Blackness is a wound that any Latinx of color experiences. I say this because racism against people of color is informed by the idea that dark-skinned people are backwards and savage. Racism necessitates anti-Blackness, as Blackness was marked "unhuman" during slavery. This mark of unhuman facilitates racism and colorism, which people of color experience. However, non-Black people of color do not experience anti-Blackness. In fact, they may perpetuate anti-Blackness, which maintains the controlled image of Blackness and melanin as "bad." Because people of color have melanin and live as racialized subjects, an investment in anti-Blackness is an investment in the very root of why they experience racism and colorism. Therefore, the liberation of all Latinx people of color necessitates the liberation of Black Latinxs. If this does not happen, systems of racism, colorism, and anti-Blackness will prevail in the Latinx community.

MEXICAN WHO SAYS N████A

But we're the same! It's all reclamation, nigga!

(Costa Rican, the half Black, frustrated that his black boxes keep failing him, gets up from his seat, drink empty but gripped by angry fists. The Dandelions freeze, hope to pretend to ignore an impending fight, but will not be afraid to call the cops should their fragile heads risk blowing away in the fray.)

COSTA RICAN, THE HALF BLACK

N██a, we are not the same!

FRANTZ FANON

Confronted with a world configured by the colonizer, the colonized subject is always presumed guilty. The colonized does not accept his guilt, but rather considers it a kind of curse, a sword of Damocles.

Speaking of swords, y'all ever play *The Legend of Zelda*??

(Snaps fingers. The reverberations pry wallflower eyelids open like manhole covers pouring sunlight into sewers. Three brown dots sit back down, avert violence they'd been causing one another for so long. They listen to Cuban with Pontiac's bandage; Dandelions exhale in relief that they no longer have to worry about doing any work tonight.)

It's, like, every game is the same: You get through all of these obstacles and you're finally at the last boss. You fight the last boss. You beat the last boss. The last boss gets back all lost health. Then you end up fighting the same monster—a bigger version; the real monster—with your health now drained to the last drop!

DANDELIONS [*NAMES REDACTED. ETHNICITY WITHHELD*]
(Poise off stage)
[We] know exactly what you [all] are talking about!

(Exeunt reticence of still flowers. Enter confidence of Dandelions thrilled to twist the tense air, steer it into video games to speak common loser languages, to drown seeds of empathy with top-shelf tequila. To revel in mainstream rejection.

Enter noise that grows large and with teeth, like a polar bear on hind legs, as spores float around the room and douse everything in pearl painted petals. Emphasizes the brown in the eyes of the three brown dots. Hides them. Makes them believe they are the color of shit. Makes them swear the dandelions are not weeds. Three brown dots. Names redacted. Ethnicity withheld.)

Coda

Scene

Long Beach, CA.

Sometime in the late 2010s, when Costa Rican, the half Black child should know better. He has never returned to South Gate, considers himself free from locked doors.

The Players:
• COSTA RICAN, THE HALF BLACK CHILD, who is now an adult. Has a bachelor's and a master's degree in English; therefore, he understands words better than many. For instance, in this scene, he is with his partner—defined as a significant other, spouse, date, long-term relationship, fuck buddy, what have you. Here, she is a girlfriend with a PhD in Ethnic Studies. She is tuned in perfectly to politically correct language, to marginalized histories, to decolonizing marginalized communities. Before we start the scene proper, hear her correct Costa Rican, the half Black child, warning to say "unhoused" rather than "homeless." She grew up in Southeast LA in a city neighboring South Gate, where years of anti-Black rhetoric doused her journey, lessons taught by Latinx elders trying to find place while cowering behind locked doors. They were told by the whites, shortly before flight, "The Blacks will rob you. The Blacks will take food directly from your mouths," all the while weeds grew over their property—forced to rip them from the ground by hand, the weeds continue to grow in defiance of beautification. This haunted her, and now she makes sure everything is correct to banish the ghosts.

[Acknowledgments—despite her importance to this narrative, witness Dr. PartnerGirlfriend's absence from the PLAYERS list. Her voice made tangible and locked away. One can transform life into a stage play to control the actor's mouths, to unlock the thoughts of others one is so desperate to know, but the actors will always reinterpret the writer's emotions to understand them as their own. I want to make sure Dr. PartnerGirlfriend does not sin like the elders, so I must lock her voice away. I am so sorry.]

- BLACK MAN, THE BLACK MAN, exists. Twenty something. Dressed to the nines in a black leather jacket lined with leopard print, high-top sneakers ripe with gloss, and a backpack signifying he has somewhere to be.

(Look—midday. A strip mall bustles with a diverse set of shoppers who will soon be witnesses. A Jack in the Box flanks jewelry stores, and Dr. PartnerGirlfriend parks her car in front of an eyebrow threading shop run by several Asian women. Costa Rican, the half Black child, a full adult, waits for her as she enters the salon.)

COSTA RICAN, THE HALF BLACK CHILD
(Sits in the passenger's seat, waiting with doors unlocked, looking at the audience)

My partner tells me threading her eyebrows will only take five minutes at most. She left the keys in the ignition, and I sit in the passenger's seat answering texts or scrolling through Instagram. I "Like" and "Share" all the social justice posts I can, made easy when sealed inside a mostly new Toyota SUV. The car doors are not locked, and I only notice that when I catch sight of a Black man coming around the corner.

(Visible to Black Man, the Black man, Costa Rican, the half Black child leans over to the ignition and double clicks the lock button,

setting off the lights and a noisy beep. Seconds later, Black Man, the Black man walks over to the passenger seat window and knocks.)

BLACK MAN, THE BLACK MAN
I saw you do that. I don't appreciate you acting like I'm a threat.

COSTA RICAN, THE HALF BLACK CHILD
(Said sheepishly, almost dismissive)

My bad.

(Black Man, the Black man continues to reprimand the half Black child's locked doors. In low shouts, he calls half Black child, "nigga," a few times. This is all half Black can hear.)

COSTA RICAN, THE HALF BLACK CHILD
(Said small, afraid, now a husk)

I'm sorry, I'm so sorry.

BLACK MAN, THE BLACK MAN
You talkin' too fuckin' low, nigga. I can't understand you. You think I'm tryna steal your car? Just cus I'm walkin' too close for your comfort? Man, you a little bitch. And I can tell you Black, too. I can tell you mixed. But I know that's yo' white side that did that shit, nigga. Grow the fuck up.

(Exeunt Black Man, the Black man. Enter air thick with sin. Costa Rican, the half Black child almost chokes on it as though pollen bit into his lungs like ticks. Instead, he looks at us again.)

COSTA RICAN, THE HALF BLACK CHILD
I'm sorry, man! That's what I would have said if I got out the car. I would try to tell him It was a reflex! *I would lock the door on*

literally anyone. Even my own Pops, who's also Black. Wait, I mean, my Mamá, and she's not white. I'm not white! Should I speak Spanish to you? I only know so much but know I'm not white. I beg you: take my blood test now, and you'll see that I am your ally. I am you. I can bring you air if you suffocate. I can give you my lungs.

(beat)

None of that happens outside of my imagination, then my partner comes back with fresh eyebrows. Rather than tell her what just happened, I try to joke with her, ask her what Latinas' obsessions are with getting pampered at Asian beauty spots. I ask because Mamá indulges, too.

(beat)

Partner and I do laundry at a spot next to a boba cafe. I get green tea and she warns me not to leave my things alone at the laundromat for too long, as there is a large unhoused community that walks in and out of the unsupervised laundry space. While folding my clothes, I see a white schizophrenic yelling into the air as he walks past the wide-open back door of the laundromat.

(beat)

The door is held open by a single brick surrounded by grass growing out of the concrete. I want to take the brick and hold it. I want the door to slam shut like an atom bomb kissing the Earth.

(beat)

Oh, Dandelions: such poxes on perfect gardens. Weeds allowed more shelter than the unhoused. How easily they can be dispatched with a single breath, how easily that breath becomes a monster for destroying beautiful weeds. I instead bite my tongue, the taste of blood locks inside my mouth, washes my teeth with silence: a language all at once universal and violent.

(Exeunt ~~Costa Rican, the half Black child and Dr PartnerGirlfriend~~ Names redacted. Ethnicities withheld.)

Judy Garland in Blackface

Dear J [ ],

You hated it every time I called you "famous." Said you were a daughter of Ojai, CA, and only played enough gigs to pay electricity bills. Your Tinder photo, however, convinced me that your name fit well on marquees and that you had a voice powerful enough to illuminate moons: the background an electric white, you sat with a semi-hollow electric guitar—an auburn burst Ibanez—firm on your lap, the strap slung across your shoulder like a hitchhiker's bag. Your hair caught in the wind, the curls cascading away from the camera to better show the vivid olive skin accentuating sundry shades of both your mother and father.

The photo was very punk. You didn't get that the first time I told you. I tried rescuing the comment, mentioning you had Sister Rosetta Tharpe vibes. Her voice was powerful, just like yours. I wish I could have shown you how she performed "Didn't It Rain?" in 1964. She belted out *my angel's got the key and ya can't get in* with ferocity and without a microphone—everyone heard her clear even in actual rain as she casually strolled on a wet floor, big fabulous coat and golden hair, strumming a white Gibson SG to a roaring audience hypnotized by her confident Black hands. I wish I had her hands; they knew work and melody: they knew how to hold an audience's gaze the way *she* dictated. But all you said was, "Oh, I *think* I've heard of her." I moved on, doubling down on your fame, noting your Tinder picture, if nothing else, looked like a promotional photo for an upcoming single *by* an up-and-coming single. I don't remember if you laughed at puns, and I apologize if you don't.

I fear being pretentious. Growing up an Afrolatino punk, I become very protective of things I know make me feel whole. Sometimes this doesn't include Black things, or Latino things, earning scorn from friends who don't understand my niches. One coined the term *nega-nigger* because I wouldn't fall in line with Black stereotypes.

"You don't like watermelon, you don't eat fried chicken," a non-Black high school friend once accused, "You don't do anything a real Black person does."

I lie to myself and say those words didn't destroy me, keeping those memories at bay until I figured out how to be secure in my apparent Black and brown mutation. Seeing your guitar and your mixed skin made me believe you had figured out how to not see yourself as a defect, but an evolution. I became jealous; needed to become your student.

At the time we matched, I adjuncted at community colleges. Teaching composition, I pretended to be at a 10, feigning excitement and energy; pretended I had the same energy teaching as playing punk shows. On stage, I also have to be at a 10. Punk calls for release, to let othering disintegrate into noise, so every show we play has to be violent. No one gets hurt, don't get me wrong. Punk allows me to surrender to the anger. I aim it at whites, make noise louder than my own voice could otherwise handle. Of course, this is only some nights. Most of the time, I grade papers written by some white kid who really did not like *The Bluest Eye*.

Your job is music. God, I wanted that. One of the first things I said to you was how starstruck I was; you made money gigging at wine bars, Irish pubs, and courtyards in your hometown. Even in Ojai, where I quipped, "Isn't that where rich white people are invented?" your performances were respected. How could I not admire that?

Bludso's Bar & Que lives in the halfway point between Ojai and Long Beach, so we agreed to meet up there for a quick "get to know you" dinner and beer for our first date. On the drive, I listened to Janelle Monáe's *The ArchAndroid* front to back. I figured you would enjoy her stylings as much as I did, hoped her sound was a nice middle ground when the topic of music came up. Punk, I felt, was a lost cause, and my ardent disdain for Jason Mraz and Jack Johnson would not complement your admiration for their styles. But I wanted to ask about how much you loved Monáe; her fashion, her dance moves, her lyrics in "Cold War" where she exclaims, *I'm trying to find my peace / I was made to believe there's something wrong with me / . . . this is a cold war—do you know what you're fighting for?*

The rain hadn't started yet, so I walked inside dry as a bone. Your hair was a giveaway, full and coiled, covering your face as you sat alone on a bench with a blonde ale. You recognized me immediately, getting up to give me a hug. This was our first interaction in person, smiles and embraces, as though we knew each other already. You wore a vibrant Marvel sweater, and I wore a muted black-and-gray plaid button up. We talked about the drive, then movies and comic books. We did not talk about Janelle Monáe.

I get the tri-tips and mac and cheese, and you school me on the differences between The Avengers' *Civil War* comic book versus the movie. I keep a real smile going until my stout is empty and the last bite of my tri-tip is in my stomach. After I did my best not to rant about why Christian Bale's Batman voice gets too much flak, we called it. Altogether, the first date lasted two hours, and I managed to keep my pretensions at bay like a rabid dog in a muzzle, hoping you understood my *Simpsons* references, praying you wouldn't quote *Milk and Honey.*

When we left Bludso's, it started to rain. Since we both parked in the pitch-black back-alley neighborhood a few blocks from Bludso's, I walked you to your car. You intentionally stepped in puddles with the protection of rain boots, and you let water drizzle into your hair. Your coat didn't have a hood, but you happily let your hair—bursting with curls, unapologetically Black—drink the water. My dreadlocks were barely a month old, concealed with a tightly fastened bandana to avoid air, bugs, heat, and white people's hands, so I was amazed by your bravery letting your hair breathe despite the hazards of Earth.

We walked on the street itself and finished our conversation about comics. Your car was a quaint, white sedan. Maybe a little older than my car, and something that had seen its share of miles. I expected some form of Mercedes or an Audi fresh off the lot, but I guess even the most famous musicians tend to stick to beat up touring vans. I didn't say any of this to you because it sounded stupid. You kissed me on the cheek and drove back to Ventura.

The second date came about a week later when you gifted me a whole day of your presence. This time, we met up in Glendale to eat lunch at Porto's, where I swore by their potato balls. We sat in the center of rush hour, bodies coming in and out, standing in massive lines to order food and pastries. Many of them disgruntled. Regardless, you smiled unfazed. You wore boots again, designer this time. Your black jeans and red sweatshirt let you meld into the crowd; let you drink in anonymity like lemonade.

You picked at your Cubano sandwich but swore you enjoyed the food. Despite the pleasant start to this date, we started our first real conversation of that day talking politics, nearly against our will. Trump had been inaugurated in the week between dates, so we couldn't help but vent. I told you about my white ~~allies~~ friends who refused to vote for Clinton after Bernie was out of the race, you told me about the red voters in your city being vocal about swallowing pride in order to cast a republican vote in November— how backwards it should have been, we joked.

But it was through our disgruntled political chat that music finally came out of our mouths. You told me about performing protest songs the day of the Women's March. Driving down to LA was out of the question, so some music friends of yours got together in Ojai to talk about freedom, to tell each other that you were all visible in a crowd of angry Americans, to play songs and remember your voices still worked. In Ojai, people knew your name from marquees around the city, so to know you were using *that* name, the [   ] name, to spread peace of mind to people who all lost safety on the same night was a beautiful thing. When I said that, you didn't cringe. Whether you embraced the fame, or were numb to it, you soaked in my allusion to your widespread appeal. You smiled. Maybe this was flirting.

Outside Porto's, D.A.R.E. asked us to donate. Normally I walk right past those tables—I don't hate charities; my anxieties simply intensify being broke and unable to give to said charities. You are much more extroverted, had much more money in your pockets, so you welcomed their requests, signed away a few bucks without issue. One of the helpers kept me company while you signed things. Asked me how my day was, asked me what we had planned and hoped it was nice. Then asked if you were my sister.

Had he been a white guy, I would have chalked it up to some microaggressive ignorance and dumb curiosity. But he was a Black guy who saw past my light skin and into the texture of my baby dreads, the shape of my face, the tone of my voice; saw bodies born from Black ancestry, and he recognized our identities without question. Nothing *nega* about it. On a romantic level, a mood killer. When you finished, he and I ended our brief conversation, and I said nothing about how he confused us for siblings.

You remember, I know, going to the Museum of Contemporary Art shortly after. You remember consolidating our cars at Griffith Park, how I drove us to the museum while trying (and failing) to keep my cool with LA traffic. I couldn't tell if my brief outbursts against drivers impressed you or would be the eventual deterrent, but I cursed at them with comfort. I cursed at them knowing you were on my side of these nonverbal arguments. Nonetheless, the comfort in the car opened my mouth when my iPod sang on shuffle.

"Any requests?" I asked, and you said the music was fine—good even—and asked about the artist. You said you dug the soulful singing juxtaposed with a sample of Fred Hampton's "I Am A Revolutionary" speech.

"Algiers," I said, naming the band, playing them up as "that Black Lives Matter type music." I mentioned how important it was to have a Black person front a punk band with biting social commentary that's also commercially viable for a wider audience. This was more *me* than I hoped to show on a second date: melodiously prejudiced, transforming musical notes into a pretentious dissertation. You didn't seem to mind.

"This is punk?" You asked. "Doesn't sound very punk."

It's hard to translate how difficult it was for me to not talk your ear off about real punk, to not catalog Bad Brains and Alice Bag's entire biography for you, to not espouse the anti-racist rhetoric of punk started by people of color but lost to white punks who stole the genre, to not talk about how seeing the big textured hair on Cedric Bixler-Zavala and Omar Rodríguez-López of At the Drive-In convinced me that there was room on this planet for an Afrolatino like myself. I let the mantra of "She doesn't care, she doesn't care, she doesn't care," echo inside my sedan.

"Punk can be a lot of things," I conceded. "But this is definitely a good version of it."

Part of my anxieties is the oscillating fear of not saying enough in a public forum and the fear of saying too much. Before I could spiral into a bottomless well of esoteric bands you'd never remember, I asked, "Who do you like? Who influences the great J?"

You laughed off the fame. Said Judy Garland.

"Her voice is so pure," you said. "I grew up watching *The Wizard of Oz*. Dorothy's unbreakable innocence, the stars in her eyes illuminated in color *and* monochrome. *She* made me want to create music. I have other favorites, of course, but *she* just always leaves me shook."

If you had seen my tongue at that moment, you would have seen my taste buds lined with teeth marks. I wanted, badly, to ask if you had seen the movie *Everybody Sing*. Judy Garland struts out in complete blackface—southern Black girl ponytails sticking in every direction, her arms and face painted the color of tar, those lips painted to make her own mouth appear three times its normal size to draw attention to her singing. She sings a jazzed-up version of "Swing Low (Sweet Chariot)," turning the tune from a negro spiritual into a family friendly jingle. She did jigs, worked the shoulders, got the facial expressions down. This is the Judy I think about, innocence like broken glass.

I understand Ms. Garland was fifteen when she did that movie, three years prior to *The Wizard of Oz*. Had drugs forced onto her, several levels of abuse from parents and powerful men alike, all of which culminated in multiple suicide attempts. I understand that no one has a handle on who they are or should be at fifteen. I understand that the '30s gave enough space to blackface to weaken its position as a racist act, normalizing the dehumanization of Black folk. If anything, movies like *Everybody Sing* or *The Jazz Singer* saw blackface as an act of rebellion by the white person singing the negro's jazz. Judy's character—Judy—used the song and dance to discover herself, using "subversive" arts to entertain within her means. Being fifteen and a hungry actress means saying yes to a lot of things. I understand that this role is rarely, if ever, talked about in a positive light when discussing her career, but I don't know how to forgive her. No matter how forced they were into the role.

So, should I believe she truly hated racism later in life? She got so much praise for being a fierce proponent of the queer community around the time *A Star is Born* revived her career in later years. Her minstrel act became forgotten by the mainstream like a bad hairdo. But I can't forget the sound of applause for Judy Garland in blackface. Maybe that's why I like punk so much—makes me feel less othered for screaming all the time.

What is your secret, J? Why do you forgive? How do you pardon such thrashings to your bloodline? Did you learn something about your identity that I didn't? Was it easy?

What *is* your secret?

At MOCA, you wouldn't tell me—luckily, I didn't ask, instead deciding to swim in my own repressed crises, fighting to keep my pretentions and academic tongue stifled, fighting to not tear down the Garland statue firmly risen in your head. Instead, we wandered the museum, paying loose admiration to the art as we walked a steady distance from one another. Every now and again, we'd look at a piece together, make a *Simpsons* joke or two, but we walked at our own paces, only slightly differing in speed.

There was a single picture in my phone that I took of you: we walked into a hallway of wall-to-wall art, words on the ceiling, figures on the floor, and you snapped a photo of the words above you because they inspired you. You wanted to keep them forever without removing a piece of the roof, and I wanted to capture your movements to hold your innocence still forever. Forgive me, I don't remember the words you loved because the photo is no longer on my phone. But I do remember you told me they reminded you of your grandfather.

"My grandfather once killed a man," you said, still smiling as we started walking at equal pace exiting the museum. "I don't think he's a bad person. He can't be. People tried to lynch him, and he just plain didn't want to get lynched. He wanted to live. Didn't want to be picked out of a group for being different. No one does. Sometimes my mom talks about it with shame, as though killing someone threw dirt on our name. I admit that it's a famous name, but my grandfather didn't dirty it up. He fought back and got away. Got to live. It's not a crime to live."

We walked through the streets of Downtown LA keeping pace with one another, talking about more comics and movies, both feeling guilty about our excitement for the Power Rangers movie reboot. We stopped at a bar for a beer and stories. I told you about the few times I had been in the Ventura area, mostly for punk shows and pizza at Jimmy's Slice. Still, I had never been in Ojai proper. Celebrities live there, as you know. You've seen Britney Spears around town, you've bumped into Tom Selleck. Close to the beach, secluded, the perfect town for anonymity, for taking breaks from spotlights and such.

You graduated from a private high school in a class of about twenty people. A healthy mix of mostly white kids, some Asian kids, and a few brown kids, you also felt the sting of Black absence. No matter: you said everyone was nice, and the intimacy kept your teen years calm and the angst tempered. You laughed when I told you about my graduating class of over 100 kids in a public school of about 4,000 Latinos. This was a claustrophobia you couldn't understand, but it trained my lungs to breathe when given only so much space.

Ojai's general population of about 8,000 paled in comparison to South Gate's 90,000. Your town housed retired white liberals, guarded by views of forests and water. It's where I imagined the whites flew to when they abandoned South Gate. They took the money, the resources, the care for the ground we all walked on— ground that sprouted at least one more pothole every day the sun came up. Whites left us to pick up their trash. My high school amplified this by cramming all the leftover students into woodshop, metal shop, and other trade classes; all reminders to grow up as worker bees to make white life more convenient.

Regardless of the malaise, the despair, the abandonment, I told you about my hometown. You thought it was funny because I wanted you to think it was funny. I made my city to be sardines and not prisoners; I can't even do that for myself. But you knew what it meant to be a mixed kid. Remember we were both the only Black kids in our classes; remember the solidarity in your laughter when I told you the *nega-nigger* stories. Remember the laughter disintegrating the words, our Black laughter, making *nega* impotent in anyone else's mouth. Maybe we just got used to being othered, and the laughter came to help us breathe a better pace. Then, with more alcohol, we joked about other terrible things. Laughing about the possibilities of the world coming to an actual end as the cherry on top of 2016. All we needed was extinction to make everything make sense. A fresh start, an asteroid to collide with the Earth to turn everything into ash—to weld us all together as a single pile of seared dust and travel in scattered directions by wind. The cracks in the gravel, the exploding bark of trees, the crashing oceans, the collapsed peoples, the chorus of screams, you said, would make an excellent song.

"It'd be the last great punk song," you said, then we laughed, and laughed, and laughed, our cackles in sync as though Armageddon had already soldered our voices together.

At the end of the second date, it did not rain despite the night clouds. We each had long drives home, so I took you back to your car at Griffith Park—we were both shocked the traffic was gone, and I was secretly shocked your car had yet to be towed. I vocalized how I talked too much, but you waved it off, said I kept you entertained with the stories. So, we planned to go to the movies soon, once my semesters started and I could figure out my teaching schedule, how to go about meeting up among all the essays I had to grade and traveling I already had to do as an adjunct. You wanted to see *Power Rangers*. I wanted to see *Power Rangers*.

Your lips landed on mine—even if only briefly—as a sign of thank you, of appreciation, of "my car is still here, hooray," of adhering to the status quo of date protocol, of physically telling me you had a nice time. In that kiss, however, I knew there would be no romance. Maybe it's that idea of chemistry people go gaga over and the lack thereof, but there was a finality to your kiss. You drove back to Ventura, and I went back to Long Beach. We texted here and there the weeks following, but more time passed between texts. Plans became hazier, blanketed. "Let's see *Power Rangers*" turned into "let's catch a movie" turned into "let's catch up," then nothing.

You will never read this. I hope. Besides, I've run out of stamps. I used to have plenty—bought a packet of a "Legends of '60s Pop Culture" with [   ] on it, your namesake. Wanted to make sure, if I sent letters to anyone, they understood Blackness as the apex of pop culture for *at least* fifty years. Anyway, those stamps are gone now. I never even learned your exact address despite our promises to visit each other's cities, or to see each other perform.

Still, I write this letter simply to say, again, I am jealous. Specifically, jealous of your hands. They know work, they know song, they are voluntarily calloused to birth the melodies you sing every night for sustenance. Everyone sees your fingers walk like river water. They see the Black, the white, a perfect synthesis of bones existing despite any violent histories. Your hands dance as proof your grandfather survived.

At the time I write this letter, I don't play punk as much as I wish. I don't get to scream as much as I used to. My work clothes cover up my tattoos, my skin, my callouses. These days, my dreadlocks reach past my shoulders, but I still reign them in with hair ties to please my bosses, to not scare the students. I don't play guitar as often as I used to, and now my fingers are weak and afraid of paper cuts. But, also as I write this letter, know that I am trying to find the music again, the wholeness that punk promised me all my life.

For now, I am jealous, but I am happy. Thanks to social media, I know you've played more shows in LA and shook more hands in the industry. The happiness you wear is tangible in the photos of bigger theaters and fuller audiences. It almost makes me regret never seeing you perform, even when I had chances; to see you use your voice to silence a room full of people who think they know you better than you do, to get white people to clap along at your will. Hell, you could summon rain to pour over everyone and everything, but you would swim in the flood. I know that, when you perform in front of spellbound eyes, you are not J, the girl from the dating app that ate tri-tip and explained Marvel's *Civil War* to me.

No, no, no.

You are J.

Daughter of Ojai.

The Black Judy Garland.

Descendant of [   ].

Heir of Sister Rosetta Tharpe.

Later, you married a woman who makes you feel complete. I only know through social media—you've since removed me from your "follows," something I didn't realize until after I saw the wedding photo posted of the both of you in white, sitting on a large, decorative crescent moon. Your hair tied to reveal your face for the photo, a rejection of the idea that you need to hide your Blackness. You kiss your wife's white face like forgiveness.

The photo is very punk. You hold your wife's hand, sharing your wounds with her, trusting her with fingers that dance like water. That trust comes in *handy*; I'm told. I still don't remember if you liked puns. Maybe you did, and I'm the one who doesn't like puns. I don't know. Maybe I'm just pretentious, but puns are dumb. I never understood why something that exists as more than one thing is supposed to be funny.

Sincerely,
M

The Assassination

of the Coward Red

January 21st, 2013

Red wants to play some songs, or he might kill himself. He'd
written ten songs, said nine of them are good. Today was the
first time we'd spoken in a month, the first friend I've casually
talked to outside of the master's program. We ate shitty Quiznos
subs in the school's food court as he talked about the band. A
three piece: me on guitar, him on bass and vocals, and a drummer he swears he will find. Red let slip that I was the second
person he asked to play guitar.

He probably still had reservations about me since our previous band fell out. Red hated playing in that band: the marathon
jams, the songwriting, the control I had over our direction. We
disbanded, and he hopped around from failed band to failed band
while I finished my bachelor's degree and moved on to an MFA.
The original guitarist Red wanted was his childhood best friend in
San Diego. Unfortunately, his childhood best friend in San Diego
didn't want to drive from San Diego to LA and back for practice
three times a week.

Today, Red said he needed my help. Said he needed me on guitar
to bring the songs to life. My lips held in, "You couldn't find *anyone
else?*" and "I just came here to catch up," because I know Red's
history with rejection, how he covers scars with baggy clothes, how
he cloaks his eyes with the rabid curls of his ginger hair. Red's hands
shook fearing I'd say no. Red needs these songs to make him feel
like his hands and throat have permission to exist.

February 5th, 2013

Rush Week. Frat tables and clubs littered the quad like trash. After my proseminar, I ran through the center, avoiding eye contact with students holding pamphlets. I didn't need reminders that the campus had nothing for my niches. I needed to eat.

Alone on a stone bench, I saw Red. Ginger curls and chalked skin in torn jeans and a red flannel covering his "Death to the Pixies" T-shirt. He sat with his eyes to the ground, his shoulders spiked above his head, frigid with fear that someone would talk to him. I walked up, my dark brown afro, my skin slightly darker, hoping familiarity would thaw him.

Red is the president of the campus' Underground Music Society, where he helps punk bands and rappers play shows on campus on the merits of social justice. The group picked up steam over the year, young punks of color like us gravitating toward Red's brainchild. Their booth bursts with energetic nineteen- and twenty-year-olds, which scared Red.

I'm not talkative like them. I can't even stay in a band for longer than a hiccup, so what am I doing being president of this stupid club besides failing at it? Me quiero ir a casa.

Red speaks Spanish when he is nervous. His first language. Both his parents are Mexican, but a quarter of his dad's European blood made sure Red's skin and hair passed for "certified white boy." Our initial bond came from this shared guilt in having lighter skin in our communities, being gaslit into believing we don't belong. We take turns trying to tell the other one we are whole. This was my turn.

Tell me more about these songs, I said, starving.

February 6th, 2013

The band is named Culero. In Red's Mexican tongue, "coward."

February 12th, 2013

Practice today started poorly. Red recruited some white metalhead frat guy to play drums. He walked by the Underground Music Society's booth, initially stopping by to plug his own metal band. The frat guy was amused by the booth's usage of punk names, wanting one himself.

Red warned me: *I was like, "Yeah, my guitarist goes by Blacky Moose. I go by Red Chihuahua." And he immediately said, "I wanna be Iron Cobra!" and I was like, ". . . fuck it."*

Cobra and I didn't get along. When he first entered the room, he gawked at me, diagnosing my ethnicity.

You know who you kinda look like? ~~Jimi Hendrix~~
~~Lenny Kravitz~~   ~~Ben Harper~~   ~~Bob Marley~~
~~Eric Andre~~   ~~Michael Ealy~~

The way Cobra said *Blacky* made me hate punk. He also didn't chip in for the rehearsal space Red rented for two hours, claiming he was doing Red a solid just being there. He sat down behind the kit, displeased that it was a standard four-piece set-up instead of twenty, bragged about his skills accumulated from his death metal band.

I kept to my side of the space as Red doled out instructions. This mostly consisted of, *Play this part fast, and the next part the same but faster.* Between false starts, Cobra added verbal notes to Red's instructions to make the song more metal.

Trust me! My other band has thousands of followers. I know what I'm talking about.

Red sat down with his bass. Hands start with soft quivers, his body's punishment against Red's attempt at confidence. But I strummed the notes Red wanted, music crisp swimming out of the rented amplifier. Red's ears caught the harmony. He calmed his nerves by running fingers through his red mane, a slow groom. His breaths caught pace before he met Cobra's eyes.

I don't give a shit about your other band. I don't give a shit about your followers. I asked you here to play these songs. You said 'Yes.' Now play these fucking songs.

Cobra shut up. Cobra listened. The songs started coming together. We played for the rest of our allotted time, loosened muscles and bounced around the room as though playing to a club full of punks. Red screamed into his microphone, vomiting anxieties and blood curdled words that drowned in a hurricane of noise. My guitar painted the walls with fuzzed distortion. The drums became deafening assault rifles. Red gesticulated with the grace of a swan among the vicious winds, maneuvering as though escaping an egg, using his limbs for the first time. By the end of the practice, the quake of the windows settled as Red caught his breaths after the roars.

We practice again in two days.

March 4th, 2013

The band is named Culero. In Mamá's Central American tongue, "faggot."

May 11th, 2013

We've played a show a week for the past three weeks.

Show #1—A Sunday: Our first official show together. We traveled in separate cars to San Diego, close to Red's childhood home where his parents still reside. Cobra set up a show with a promoter at a pizzeria, after hours with several other bands. All of them were Tech-Death Metalcore bands with amplifiers so loud they deafened the audience, forcing people to leave little by little throughout the show. When we got there, the promoter looked at the three of us, *Wait, I thought you said you had a Black guy in your band?* After I told him I was half Black, he said, *No, I mean a real Black guy. Not two and a half white guys.* Neither Red nor I had the strength to tell him neither of us were white. Cobra apologized to the promoter, making sure we still played the show. All the other bands had exclusively white dudes, but we got the tongue lashing for not being diverse enough. We go on last, starting at 12:45 a.m., only playing four of our planned nine songs. All the bands went home before we played, even though we arrived early to support their sets. The promoter, Cobra's girlfriend, a couple of mine and Red's mutual friends, and some dude named Dylan stayed for us. Red pointed at Dylan before we played our last song.

This song's for you, Dylan!

Show #2—A Saturday: We opened a house show in the suburbs of the Inland Empire. One of Cobra's frat brother's birthdays. The sun stayed glued in the sky, blinding us, paying more attention to our set than the partiers who drank Coronas and lounged in beach chairs or bounced on a trampoline. The other bands didn't show up until after we finished. Red stayed to support them. Some white kid asked to borrow my guitar cable for his band's set.

Sorry to ask, bro. I forgot mine. Loved your set by the way!
Rather than remind him he showed up a half hour after we finished, I gave him the cable. Told him to keep it. No one noticed I left until Red texted me an hour later to ask where I was, and if another band could use my amp.

<u>Show #3—A Friday</u>: Red's friend from the Underground Music Society asked us to play an all-ages queer punk show at an art gallery near campus. Red said yes. I tried to get out of the show because none of us were queer and I didn't want to take up that space, but Red told me not to worry about it. He's never been that confident. Red even shortened his mane to a widow's peak. Cut it himself the night before. Said his curls made him sweat too much during shows.

The showrunners gave us time to play all nine of Red's songs. Every single person that came to the show, even the other bands, stood attentive to every note played. Their applause filled breaks between songs, their necks and ankles ached from dancing to Red's music. Red screamed with every muscle, ravished by the adrenaline of eyes acknowledging his existence.

His friend sang in TittyFucker, the headliners. Three piece. All of them playing in the nude, except for ski masks. Two brown lesbians on the mic and on guitar. Nonbinary drummer with penis duct taped to their abs to avoid accidental strikes. The band's ten-minute set was louder than wars, faster than bullets. The mosh pit became a whirlpool of queer youth colliding like stars. Cobra and I hung back, but Red joined the movement. Sweat cascaded into the air like water from a fire hydrant burst onto summer bodies. TittyFucker encouraged dancers to take off their clothes, too. Many obliged, especially Red, free from the eggshells he normally moshed on.

After TittyFucker's set ended, police raided the art gallery. Noise complaints from white passersby gave them permission to bruise some queers. People who weren't violently tackled scrammed. A couple of kids arrested in the nude. Cobra, Red, and I managed to escape with our instruments and Red's clothes. Red kept saying, *We fuckin' killed it out there*, naked, blissed.

May 23rd, 2013

My thesis chair asked, *Do you even remember you're in a graduate program?* when I emailed her about a fourth extension on my draft. I will need another year—an option reserved for the terminally ill or the expecting. I am neither. I am fucking up.

August 20th, 2013

My final show with Culero will be on my twenty-fourth birthday in Red's parent's backyard in San Diego. As penance for my departure, I spent all summer touring locally with the band, playing the nine songs we had recorded in a garage and distributed as burned CDs. None of the shows were empty, most of the crowds were receptive, and every set ended with our shirts drenched and spirits quenched. Red nixed band tees and opted for Hawaiian shirts, made him look even more punk screaming in rainbow colors and floral.

During a break from recording the songs, I told him I was leaving the band. Told him I wanted to focus on getting my master's degree the right way. Told him I needed a better academic year, that my passions were leading me away from music. I assured him that guitarists were a dime a dozen, especially in LA, especially nonwhite ones. After the break, he tracked vocals for the last song on the CD—he screamed so loud that his throat hemorrhaged. Blood peeked out the side of his mouth, merging with a tear drop rolling down his face.

September 14th, 2013

The backyard was pregnant with punks—mesh tops, leather, safety pins, clothes torn from class rather than fashion, makeup smeared by cheap beer, mosh pits, dust kicked up into the night by dirt and Doc Martens, a ghetto blaster sings Crass and SNFU and Killer Mike and Pure Hell and Millions of Dead Cops and Los Saicos and Little Richard and Piñata Protest between bands setting up and tearing down, banners rope around the fences like caution tape with phrases *Black Lives Matter* and *Gays Bash Back* and *Do Dope Fuck Hope* and *A.C.A.B.*, a cake adorned with pictures of cherub angels and the words *Happy Birthday Blacky, We'll miss you, xoxo*.

Close to midnight; nobody had left. No red or blue sirens came to wash away the beautiful chaos. Red's hair was gone, shaved to the skin with a razor blade. The beard he tries to grow keeps his namesake. My afro dripped over my shoulders, helped my beard and the night hide my face from everyone. I dressed up, today: black jeans, black shoes, and a black vest hugging a red dress shirt—Cobra called it my perfect funeral outfit.

We played, I was swept into the hurricane—punks blooming over Red's backyard, the fuzz became a cloud I could rest my unspoken words onto. Everyone danced. Their movements illuminated the person I want to be: troubadour for the dispirited, folk like me. How visible my heart in this hurricane. I don't want to leave these winds. Please, God, please let me die here.

When we played our ninth song, one of Red's bass strings snapped. He didn't stop. Played until the song's end, sour notes ignored by dancing punks. A second bass string snapped, and he dropped the bass to the floor, furiously yanking the last two strings. The song broke down, but that's OK. I pointed my guitar's pickups directly at my amplifier. Feedback peaked like a banshee in pain. Cobra played an endless, messy drum solo until his kit toppled over.

The punks applauded. After, I hugged Red.

He got blood on my vest when he hugged back with hands torn by bass strings.

November 23rd, 2014

~~I wonder if I should have died in Culero.~~
It's been six months since I earned my degree. My parents were happy that I stowed my gear away, trading punk rock for a semi-stable job. It's been decent teaching two sections of critical thinking ~~where white boys try to touch my new dreads~~ in Orange County, one section of basic skills ~~working for white knights who pretend to care about incarcerated Black folk~~ in Inglewood, and two sections of Freshman comp near my apartment. All the department chairs liked my idea for incorporating music into my lectures, so I am never too far away from punk in the ivory tower. Still, I daydream of joining Red and Cobra on their tour up and down the coast.

But I chose my plan B.

We keep in touch, though. Cobra snagged a janky RV from Craigslist for a little over a hundred dollars, and they were off. Culero started packing shows, selling out DIY venues in small cities. Their new white dude guitarist is inert on stage, Red told me over the phone, but his guitar playing is gigantic and its distortion suffocates a room. Their crowds are only slightly younger than ~~us~~ them: a lot of browns, a lot of Blacks, a lot of queers, a lot of kids that find themselves through Culero's songs—a fullness Red and I always envisioned; a fullness he now basks in.

Red told me the hospitality brought him to tears. They never paid for hotels since local bands offered their living room floors and home-cooked meals. Said the Samaritans wanted to protect the scene, to make sure touring bands felt safe traveling far from home while playing in basements, backyards, living rooms, RVs, and garages shared with neighbors.

At all these venues, the rules stayed standard at every show:

- No racism.
- No sexism.
- No homophobia.
- No transphobia.
- Keep the pits inclusive. (No white jocks in the front.)
- Donate what you can to touring bands—money or time, just help out.
- Clean up after yourselves.
- Help others.
- Be tender—please be tender.

Everything Red said makes me want to be there, and everything Red said reminds me that I could never be there. I feel wretched that I took a small amount of solace knowing how unkind the police were to Culero on tour as half the shows got shut down. Regardless, the music kept going, sometimes with guerilla acoustic sets inside homes at quieter volumes.

Red sent me a video of one raided show that turned into an acoustic driveway set. Kids banged on trashcans and car doors as percussion, Cobra used brushes on his kit rather than wood sticks, the new guitarist strummed a beat-up acoustic Red purchased from an elder in Tijuana. Red sang into open air. Even without a microphone, his voice carried weight. He said the video was a new song Culero readied for a new album. Catchy. People sang along despite no one ever hearing the song before. I watched the video ten times when he sent it, fuming especially seeing Cobra assimilated into the pack as though cleansed of being a frat bro. The song they played was so alien, with not one note I helped write. They played it with precision and care of second nature. This was a clean slate paved in a San Jose driveway, Red surrounded by people looking to his music for guidance. I watched the video one more time before putting my phone away for bed, the pulsation of the melody keeping my eyes open.

Yeah, life's not that bad
When you think about it
I mean, it's pretty fuckin' bad
But it's not THAT bad

I have to be up at 5 a.m. tomorrow to teach the white boys who want to touch my dreadlocks.

November 26th, 2014

 "Blacky Moose"

Tour has been magical, Blacky. Sorry for talking your ear off on the phone the other day, but I just haven't been this happy. Ever. People continue to be so giving. The homeowners in Tacoma gave our RV the works. They fixed the engine and replaced all the tires. Said it was a thank you for bringing so many people to their show. In Humboldt, I slept with this Mexican dude who had great taste in bands, who believed me when I said I was also Mexican. He didn't stop and say, "Nah!" He didn't look at my pasty skin or the red in my beard and say I didn't count. He just said, "Eres una hermosa persona." Have you heard someone say that before? I haven't. People used to stare and tell me who I'm supposed to be. But now, people stare at me because they are listening. I want to do this for the rest of my life. I don't want to go home, man. I don't want to go home.

This is what it feels like to be completely whole.

—Red Chihuahua

December 10th, 2014

Me: *Any questions about the final? This is your last shot.*
White Boi Student #7: *Yea. Deadass, yo—are you related to J. Cole?*
Me: *Any better questions?*

January 27th, 2015

[First voicemail from Red]
Yo, Blacky! It's Red. Call me back when you can. We haven't talked in a minute. Culero's about to do some cool shit.

January 28th, 2015

[Second voicemail from Red]
Yo, you good? I know you're busy with that newfangled job, but don't be dead, please.

January 29th, 2015
[Most recent voicemail from Red]
Saw you posted about how much you hated your job, so good to know you're still alive. Heard this joke at a show we played the other night, so hopefully it'll cheer you up.

This dude is playing Blackjack and is on his last few dollars. Dude ain't religious, but he's so desperate for a good hand that he starts praying. God answers him. God says, "On the next hand, you must hit, my child." Dude gets a 5 and a 2, so he hits. Gets a 7. God says, "On the next hand, you must hit, my child." Dude hits, gets a 6. Dude's at 20. Dude needs an Ace but feels it's too risky. God says, "No! you must hit. Trust in me." So dude hits. Gets a 5. Busts at 25. God says, "FUCK!"

You get it? I know you liked that. You better be laughing now.

[Postcard from Red, received a fucking hour after listening to Red's most recent voicemail]

 "Blacky Moose"

BLACKY, ANSWER YOUR FUCKIN' VOICEMAILS! jk I know you're really busy teaching and all that, but hope you can come out to a show soon. We had to get a new guitarist. Our guy didn't like touring, but we have a new guy. A Black dude! Kinda like you. Learned the songs super quick, so he's down to record the new album with us. I can't wait for you to hear these new songs, man. I finally made that tenth song good.

—Red Chihuahua

February 20th, 2015

Red called me, asked if he was taking me away from my "grown up" job. I said no, already procrastinating on grading essays. It should've been a "yes" so I wouldn't have to hear Red bray on about his fortunes. My stomach churned; I blamed turned leftovers. He wanted to know if he could email me the first mix of their album. I said sure. He did most of the talking, mentioned how strange it was working with an actual producer in a studio instead of a friend's garage. Culero had local record labels bidding for them, offering substantial recording budgets.

He told me everything about Culero's recording process. Wrote lyrics about his Mexican roots, his sexuality, the freedom of travel. He told me one song—the tenth song—took forever. The band couldn't nail the takes the way he wanted because of dead notes, flubbed strums, or drumming miscues. His voice got hoarse recoding vocals. Everyone told him the takes sounded great, but he wanted to redo everything until they were perfect. His voice gave out on take number thirty. They called it a day. Hoped for a better tomorrow. Red bawled the night away.

I smiled at their setbacks. He didn't see me do it, so maybe it never happened.

February 21st, 2015

I decide the misery I put myself in
If there's a cut on my arm, I put it there
If there's blood on my lips, I made them bleed
The only pain I have is the only pain I allow
Because I want it,
> *want it,*
> *want it,*
> *want it,*
> *want it,*
> *want it,*
> *want it,*
> *want it,*
> *want it,*
> *want it,*
> *want it,*
> *want it,*
> *want it,*
> *want it,*
> *want it,*
> *want it,*
> *want it,*
> *want it,*
> *want it,*
> *want it,*
> *want it,*
> *want it,*

want it,
want it,
want it,
want it,
want it,
want it,
want it,
want it.

June 15th, 2015

[Text to Red]
Dude. I have a mountain of essays to grade. Teaching
summer school doesn't mean I have a break, it means
I have double the work. I told you I'd let you know when
I'm free. I am not free. I have not told you I am free. Stop
asking me if I am coming to your show. Even if I wasn't
teaching, I am not going to your show. I wouldn't ask you
to watch your ex get fucked by her new guy, would I?

PS: Please, stop calling me 'Blacky' please.

[Text from Red]
It's chill, man! Work is tough. Lemme know when you
get more time. We've got shows lined up for a while.

[Text to Red]
Your not listening to me!!!

[Text to Red]
*You're

[Text from Red]
Yeah, dude! Just come to the next show. It's
booked and everything. Love u, Blacky <3

[Text to Red]
Fuck . . . send me the address.

June 16th, 2015

Cops beat me to Culero's show and raided the venue. Punks scattered like shattered glass as cop cars flooded the street outside the entrance. Some punks were caught, sat down on curbs, handcuffed on the floor. All I thought was, *This is supposed to be my goddamn day off.* I saw Cobra talking to an officer, barely trying to reason with the man. Red later told me that particular cop was their old guitarist's brother, so Cobra and the cop got distracted catching up, shooting the shit while kids got cuffed all around them. Just behind Cobra's back, in full view of his cop friend, another cop held Culero's newest guitarist face down: her hands restrained behind her back, white zip ties slicing into her wrists, her designer glasses—purchased after months of saving up money between two jobs—halved by concrete; she took a billy club to the ribs before being shoved in a car, her dark brown skin washed-out under shadows. The sirens of the car, like a bad song, faded away until she was gone. Cobra and the cop didn't move a muscle as the violence contoured around them.

Red watched frozen in grief with his fingers laced together over his shaved head, his fingernails coated in red, white, and green polish. He looked transformed, yet the same. He wore bright red overalls and a floral T-shirt, his flushed beard fully engulfed his mouth, his eyes heavy with helplessness I had not seen since he asked me to join the band in Quiznos. Red and blue lights evaporated as the last cop cars drove away. Cobra leisurely packed his drum set into the car. I walked up to Red and said, *We should all just go home, dude.*
¿Dónde?
Home.

February 8th, 2016

This is what I needed: my band is named Pipebomb! Exclamation point and all. Our bassist wants his punk name to be Upper Duck, our drummer Id y Yacht. Pipebomb! is all Duck's idea after we talked about music at an adjunct meeting in Inglewood. We had a mutual love for Dead Kennedys and A Tribe Called Quest, and he was the only Mexican in the English department. Yacht is Duck's former boss from a previous campus, an old punk and the only white guy Duck trusts. We all jammed on a Monday night after teaching; dress shirts all around, work boots, khakis. We played for thirty minutes without stopping, reading each other without lyrics. My dreadlocks tied in a ponytail eventually fell over my face—by the end of the jam, my glasses had long since flung to the floor. I thought I felt a cool San Diego breeze and a stage beneath me, like Culero's first show, like my last, but I wiped the sweat from my eyes and saw we were still in LA, locked inside a rehearsal space paid for by the hour. We will meet Mondays, and write songs between grading essays.

April 16th, 2016

I sent Red our five-song EP, recorded by a local producer he recommended. The first mix. Red emailed back, *Goddamn, I missed your guitar!* and nothing else.

June 16th, 2016

About thirty people came to Pipebomb!'s tenth show. I recognized fifteen of them, and three were my students. A lot of them older white dudes, but a crowd is a crowd. Some started pits, but two people miscommunicated—the white dude caught an elbow from a Black teen. The white dude shoved the Black teen face first into a wall. Despite his face being caked in crimson from the slam, the Black teen took a swing or two or three or seven at the white dude, connecting blows when necessary. The white dude threw a kick at the Black teen's sternum, then the Black teen's own elbow collided with the white dude's face, slicing open a cheek. The rest of the thirty pulled them apart like boxers at weigh-in. We stopped playing. I got on the microphone and threw a pointed finger at the white dude like a knife.

You started this shit, so get the fuck out of here! Always coming here to us, where we're trying to live. Fuck you! You're not welcome in this space. You destroy and destroy until we have nowhere else to exist. Fuck you, asshole!

The white dude flipped me off and left the venue. We played two more songs, but my energy faded, distracted by the Black blood running down the dented wall.

August 14th, 2016

Red got Pipebomb! on a bill with Culero. A punk-rock themed coffee shop by day, punk venue by night—pending the manager's day off. The show peaked at about a hundred punks crammed into the coffee shop: queer punks, brown punks, Black punks, friends of punks, parents of punks giving them rides, children of punks, employees of the shop slipping in some overtime. Everyone's eyes glued onto the instruments. The space only allowed for minimal movement, keeping bodies faced directly toward the music.

I wore a pink short-sleeve button up with roses stamped all around the fabric, tight black jeans, and Chucks. Duck wore all-black everything, his chest adorned with *Pig Destroyer*'s logo, his hair dripping with Suavecito pomade. Yacht had come from work, wore the dress shirt, the work boots, the khakis. Our distortions made the windows dance. My playing hypnotized the bobbing heads of the jumping crowd. Between songs, feedback muted the crowd's applause, but their smiles became neon lights. We were loud, we were the loudest.

But then we watched Culero. Cobra pounded his kit with gnashed teeth, their newest guitarist's digits danced up and down their Les Paul with frantic gesticulations, and Red was Red. Face drowned in eye shadow and blush, the ceiling light caked his baldness. The bass strings trembled as though ravenous for notes, the ground shaking with punk tremors. The red flower screen printed on his black shirt offset the bright green gym-shorts hoisted up his white legs. The Mexican flag hung from his amp waved from the sound of his music. As they played their last song—the tenth song—I realized this was my first time watching Culero play. As Red jumped up and down, below his feet was the Red I first met—a quiet, straight, unsure shadow. That Red has a hole in his heart from a six-shooter, gun smoke pluming from the new Red's trigger finger. This was the only violence he welcomed: the assassination of his broken self, the painful rebirth of his identity louder than guitars.

October 14th, 2016

Rather than grade midterms, I grabbed a burger with Red at a Ma and Pa near our old alma mater. He was in town for the first time in a couple months, back from a lengthy tour across the country. We sat in a booth with cracked seats near a window where white people passed by and stared at us—punks, the dreads, the ginger beard.

Red's shine had dimmed. His clothes were still showy and bright, but he looked drained. He strained to pick up his burger, but his scabs had turned into scars enough for me to believe his mental health wasn't dipping. No, he was just tired. So tired. Calloused and aching. Red told me, *Honestly, the show with you guys was the last good show we've played. Tour took a shit pretty early on. Our guitarist crashed through a wall during our set in Oklahoma—they literally left an outline of their body like it was fucking Looney Tunes. The dude hosting us said it was all good, but we didn't feel comfortable staying in their house that night. We had enough energy to drive to the next town before stopping at a hotel.*

Halfway to the next city, we hit a storm. The horizon was pitch black, and lightning bolts gave us brief glimpses of a tornado in the distance. It looked like an angry titan; a thousand feet tall, ready to eat the RV alive. Cobra made a judgement call to turn the car around and drive until we could at least see the sky again. We parked on the side of the freeway and slept for as long as we could. We woke up to smoke. Some spark went off, or a wire finally gave out, I don't even fucking know. I opened my eyes and saw the RV's roof directly above me completely covered in fire. For at least five seconds, I thought I was legitimately in hell. We all rushed out of the van and tried to save as many things as possible, pero no pudimos salvar todo. Cobra lost all his sticks. Our guitarist lost their strings and some of their clothes. The Mexican flag burned right off my amp, just before the knobs and input melted into one another. The RV caved in and turned to ash. I asked if everyone was ok, and our guitarist said "no."

And I said, "'No?' I wasn't prepared for you to say 'no.' I don't have an answer for 'no!'"

Eventually an ambulance came, then some cops. A cleanup crew took our van away. We cancelled the next show. Our guitarist wasn't recovering so we had to cancel another one. We rented a U-Haul van to carry the rest of our stuff to the next city. One morning, I did vocal exercises and couldn't scream. Every time I tried, I coughed and thought about that one time my throat bled. Got too scared to try again. My scream was gone. We canceled the rest of the tour.

January 19th, 2017

No one has seen Red since Culero broke up. He last texted that he was moving back to San Diego with his parents to figure out his next move. I can respect that. He wrote me, *Looking forward to Pipebomb!'s new shit. Send it to me when it's done. I wanna hear it.* I need to text him back.

Maybe I'll tell him Pipebomb! has long since plateaued—we're so busy with our day jobs that we turn down more shows than we play. ~~When I do pick up a guitar, I strum for walls that blindly hold my bachelor's and Masters' degrees. These days, I still daydream of San Diego nights. At home, I let my hair loose, some locks strum my spine with their length. They say hair keeps growing after death. Sometimes I stand in the mirror in those black shoes, black jeans, and black vest over a red dress shirt. Still fits. Maybe even better.~~ Maybe I'll tell Red I have been especially swamped after being hired for a full-time gig at the Orange County campus last semester. Maybe I'll tell him I daydream in class about playing music; distracts me when the students do independent work, distracts me from the world outside the classroom. I daydream about locking up, driving out, letting down my hair with Yacht and Duck. Even just practicing, the bliss I feel playing guitar nourishes me. ~~But I do wonder if I could've felt this satiation sooner by staying in Culero. Then again, maybe I would've ended up ashes on a highway.~~

January 21st, 2017

[Letter from ~~Red~~ Chihuahua]
Moose,
At our last show together, I heard you introduce yourself without the "Blacky" part of your punk name. So, if you don't mind, I'll drop it, too. I don't even like "Red" anymore. No more "Red," please. Yuck. Moving on. Red's dead, baby. Red's dead.
I thought I lost music. I didn't. Punk will always be my first love, but I couldn't do Culero anymore. It gave me enough. I drove all the way to my parents' house in San Diego, but I am not there right now. As soon as I got there, I took out my Tijuana guitar and none of my luggage, then walked away. All my possessions, my car, other clothes, my phone, sitting in the driveway of my parents' house. (Don't worry. I wrote them a letter before I wrote you, told them I'll be back when I need to be back.) I walked on the side of highways and down city streets, strumming my guitar and singing corridos. Every now and again, people gave me money for food or tip. Some had requests, and I accommodated most of them. Most people asked for Chente. He hates the gays, but so many people asked me with such enthusiasm. My fingers knew what to do:

Por tu maldito amor.
No puedo terminar con tantas penas,
quisiera reventarme hasta las venas
por tu maldito amor.
Por tu maldito amor.

I just wanted people to like me.

171

After a couple of days wandering up and down San Diego, I saw the border. It's less than an hour drive from my parent's place, but I had only seen it on family trips. Never on my own power. I walked toward the invisible line, man, singing Chente and strumming a ten-dollar guitar.

I walked right through.

They didn't stop me for a passport. They didn't look at me while trying to figure out if I was escaping into America or coming back from vacation or whatever bullshit. They saw a white guy singing corridos in overalls, and I am trying so hard to not let that ease eat at me. I am trying not to look at my wrists—they've never been shackled, but they do have wounds. When I got to Mexico, I kept walking, kept strumming. I could talk to the locals in Spanish without them knowing I had anxiety in my throat. For once, my tongue holds me together.

You would like it here, and I can't wait to tell you about it in person. I want to listen to your music when I get back, too. I always love hearing you play guitar, man—so bright and loud, so unquestionably you.

Tierra

Turtledove digs her hands deeper into the dirt; she feels the earth's permission to reclaim herself. The grime under her nails become kisses from ancestors' feet, and the city dump's odor dissipates in her fervor to find her black denim jacket. Garbage slips through her fingers as her knees cake with compost. She claws the ground, removes other people's waste, aggressive swipes at soil she does not own.

Her parent's Mexican sensibilities did not want her worshipping Satan, already fearful of the punk rock she listened to throughout her teen years and into adulthood. While away for her first semester at a public Ivy League, her parents stripped small bits of nostalgia from her childhood room, tossing black metal CDs and crust punk tapes, leaving behind Selena's *Ven Conmigo* as a sole survivor of the purges. They took down posters, flyers for local shows she snuck off to in Southeast LA, took her Ouija board, black rubber bracelets, studded belts, men's ties, and threw them all into a box hidden in their attic. Whenever Turtledove came home, she noticed vital pieces of herself missing from her room. Nonetheless, she never yelled at them. She spent too much of her teen years engaged in arguments with both parents that all ultimately went nowhere. After spending some time being miserable as the sole brown and queer collegiate in her major, she swore to try and see what her parents saw without arguments, swore to do better, to respect their heritage rather than yell at them for taking her American toys. She says, "Please ask me next time," and continues to love them.

Then she came home one weekend to find the denim jacket accidentally thrown away—gifted by a lesbian friend for a birthday, adorned with queer and punk patches that awakened Turtledove.

The jacket looked small or big or dirty, whatever her parents said to soften the blow. Turtledove said nothing before leaving the house for the city dump.

She knows the dump well; a hang out spot with her other punk friends from high school, all queer women, brown and Black. They often broke into the dump to drink BuzzBallz after shows and avoid going home. One evening, as friends flooded the conversation with drunken Spanish, Turtledove found a dead bird among nearby garbage, beak protruding from the landfill like a flare. She unearthed the body, cradled it in her palms, waited for feathers to catch the wind and take the bird back into the sky. But it rotted in her intoxicated hands. Her friends laughed at the non-resurrection.

"You're Turtledove now," her friends said, teasing at first, then consoling "That's your new punk name, bruh."

Now she finds the jacket, soiled and the arms torn. She works to make the jacket more hers, harder to be seen as trash. First, she cuts the arms off completely. Then she studs silver along the stitching, to keep her body anchored. She grips the stitches whenever feet surrounding her beat the ground so loud she can't hear her own thoughts. Thread by thread, she rebuilds her identity, then wears the vest every day. To bars, to shows, to classes, to her undergraduate graduation, to her master's graduation, to her doctorate graduation, to adjuncting gigs, to conferences, to panels, to a tenure track position in American Studies, over band shirts, over floral blouses, over sweaters, over jackets, over sundresses. Every day.

*

Turtledove is surrounded by gardens and umbrellaed by trees on her wedding day. Attendees sit in chairs on the grass, and the sun shines on hers and Moose's linked hands under an altar adorned with gardenias. Turtledove's favorite flower, not just for Maria Rita's "Dos Gardenias"—one of Turtledove's favorite non-punk anthems—but for the placidity and joy soaking within the petals.

Moose gifted them to Turtledove once, early in their relationship. They lasted a while before naturally wilting. They saved two; Moose wears them as a boutonniere.

Just below their feet is stolen dirt, a morbid invitation for her distant ancestors to her wedding. Regardless, they hold one another's hands and smile, gold bands cover tiny turtle tattoos on their ring fingers. Their vows are poems; Moose putting his dusty MFA to work, Turtledove borrowing *dos gardenias para ti / Con ellas quiero decir / Te quiero, te adoro, mi vida / Ponles toda tu atención / Porque son tu corazón y el mío.*

They continue to recite these vows to one another when on the other side of the world from each other; through texts, voice notes, photos. Turtledove trusts Moose, she trusts his nonwhite pedagogy matches her own. She trusts the dissonant lyrics his all-professor punk band yells. She trusts he will do nothing but uplift her queerness. She trusts his Blackness. She trusts his brownness.

He trusts Turtledove with the anchors in his chest, the weight that sinks even on a good day. He trusts her pleas for him to seek help after he destroys a guitar in an empty bar; he trusts Turtledove will not escalate when she finds out the police try to arrest Moose even after the venue owner and an old white woman injured by the guitar decide *against* pressing charges; he trusts Turtledove just wants Moose around with feet planted rationally in the earth.

* *

Turtledove was gone during Moose's breakdown, but she was prepared for the guilt of her absence. Her flight to the conference in Hawaii was on the same night as his birthday show. The pair sat down for dinner the night before the flight. Their meal briefly derailed by an attempted break-in by someone they later identified as a disgruntled white student of Turtledove's. But, with wounds cleaned up, they reckon with their lack of surprise of the ordeal. They speak like they do every day: storytelling to make the other feel as though they were there, too. Moose apologized for texting Turtledove throughout the day about an incident at his campus separate from the Nazi student, but she assured him that she loves hearing from him, thrives in it. Turtledove told Moose all the shenanigans before her class even started.

"We knew which kid was the vandal," she started. "A Palestinian colleague received a badly written, scantily researched paper that doubled as pro-Zionist propaganda. Gave it a failing grade on technical merit alone. She told me the white kid put up a fight, called the grade racist, anti-Semitic, ignorant. She just said—among other careless errors—he misspelled his own name.

"He dropped her class. Soon after, we found file cabinets and loose papers on our floors, 'White Power' spray painted on our office doors, and all those gross MAGA hats scattered around the department like rotten easter eggs. I never told you, but one was tied to my office doorknob, basically making sure I touched the hat. The kid even left a large flag of Israel hung from my Palestinian colleague's door, probably got his buddies to plaster pornographic print outs of women in hijabs across her office.

"Today, we finally had the panel to talk about it. Filled the lecture hall in the humanities building with concerned faculty, staff, and students alike. Palestinian colleague, three other female professors, and I signed up to speak at the front table. We needed to be heard."

Turtledove starts to omit a few details to keep the peace at dinner. At the talk, she kept her phone in front, face-up in case Moose needed anything—he had mentioned needing to confront a troubled student, another Afrolatino taking advantage of Moose's racial kinship. Palestinian colleague took a seat directly next to Turtledove, wearing a black hijab tightened around her face and two adult coloring books tucked under her arms. Turtledove left out how truly annoyed she was when she saw Moose's name light up with complaints about the birthday show. She struggled to understand how that was her problem. She wanted to text back, "Buy a balloon and stay home." Instead, she ignored it.

So, of course, Turtledove does not mention this part during her dinner chat with Moose, does not mention how the light scratches of colored pencils coming from Palestinian colleague's seat also distracted her. Rather, she talks about the panel straight away. How she began with a land acknowledgement. *We would like to respectfully acknowledge and recognize our responsibility to the original and current caretakers of this land, water, and air: the Cahuilla, Tongva, Luiseño, and Serrano peoples and all of their ancestors and descendants, past, present, and future.*

As always, there was a smattering of applause from everyone in the room, the heaviest hands coming from white women Turtledove saw for the first time—excited to hear plans that will protect women, but absent from school protests for slain Black people and fights for campus restroom rights for transgender people.

Turtledove describes the talk: "The conversations start, we run down faulty safety protocols and inept security. We all share stories about white supremacy making our jobs unnecessarily taxing, and the fears that live in our bones being survivors and having to come to our own rescue. No one, to my knowledge, notices me grip my vest when the words start triggering. I just kept going. I had to."

Turtledove *does* mention the second text:

So . . . teacher advice?? That SkaterBoi kid just flipped out in my class after turning in a shitty test. Told him I'd fail him, then he threw my stuff all over the floor and jet. I just sat there. So did everyone else. I feel like I fucked up.

It gave her pause. She almost answered.

"But a white woman yelled across the room as soon as I unlocked my phone. Pointed at my Palestinian colleague and said, 'You're playing with coloring books? We need protection for our students and faculty from these monsters, and you're playing with coloring books?'

"Palestinian colleague didn't listen. She kept brushing sea creatures in blue color pencils, let her hijab graze the table while she kept her head down. I wish I had her bravery, Moose—always such sharp teeth so close to her face but she never flinches. The colors help her feel visible, the books help her cope, but there *I* was wearing everyone's anger over my vest.

"So, I fed excuses into the mic. I told the white woman we each are entitled to ride this heavy conversation differently, without outing Palestinian colleague's traumas. Of course, the white woman wasn't having it. Then a couple of white nonbinary students enter the screaming match, yelling at the white woman for not including them.

"I tried, Moose. I don't know why I felt like I needed to try, but I tried. I said, 'I'm sure she meant all femme-presenting persons,' protecting the white woman. She didn't need it, didn't deserve it from me. But I tried.

"Then I heard my Palestinian colleague speak, calm and slow, 'Just fucking expel them.' Folks stopped bickering for two seconds, like someone hit a mute button. Said, 'This is going to happen again no matter how much we pretend the university gives a shit, so let's weed these fuckers out of the school and get on with our lives.' Then she just brought her eyes back to the coloring book and added more blue to the water. I just went to class after. Lectured on white fragility and now we don't have a window."

* * *

Hope the flight wasn't terrible! Just wanted to let you know I called a therapist today. Some white dude. A hippy looking motherfucker with a gross-ass beard. Wanted me to come in today for an intake since what I told him sounded "severe." Long story short: I went, he wanted me to stay at a ""\"facility\""" like in Cuckoo's Nest. Point is, I'm heading home and am gonna look for a new person. Love you! Have fun.

Turtledove's hotel room is small and looks over the ocean, but she can't have fun. The irony of the American Studies Association holding their annual conference on Native islands keeps her stoic. "We're here now," she thinks. "Suck it up and network, I guess." From her window, she sees bars alive with tourism as white families walk around in Hawaiian shirts and leis to visit white owned businesses and buy toy tikis. Turtledove squints to see Palestinian Colleague and other friends cavorting at the bars, already drunk at 1 p.m. as they try to squeeze a vacation into a business trip.

Turtledove and three other professors and writers will speak on Chicano roquero and decolonization. Turtledove's talk draws heavily from her manuscript, *¡No Importa the Sex Pistols, Aquí Está Pónk!: On Decolonizing Punk and Eradicating Latinx Anti-Blackness.* Until then, Turtledove walks to the beach in her dress and vest, alone, doing her best to ignore the faltering cell reception as Moose tries to reach her. Near the water, she sits on a few rocks and watches the earth. Slowly, worlds apart, Moose reaches Turtledove.

Did you check in yet?

-

Let me know when you made it, yeah?

-

Sorry for all these texts. Just don't want you to worry about me. Like, just know I'm fine so you can carry on with the trip!

-

*I hope that didn't sound dismissive! Sorry if it did. What I meant was, as soon as I got home, I looked up more therapists that my insurance covers. I got options! Black folk, brown folk, people who aren't trying to lock me away for traumas they won't admit they don't understand. I'm just tryna find someone that'll prescribe a coloring book. Lol.

-

**I didn't mean that to be insensitive, either! Just, from what you told me about your colleague, it sounded like the kind of healing I'd go for, you know? Creating. Not dismantling. If she's there with you, hope she's feeling better. Please enjoy Hawaii! Try to have fun?

A giant turtle marches out of the water. Its shell a blackened green matching the seaweed and rocks. Turtledove takes a photo of the traveler, attaches it to another failed text to Moose:

My shell cannot stop
bullets
but I will still swim
To you
Before the Earth takes you home
Before my blood runs out

A little poem. A little cheesy. Sorry, not sorry. You'll find the perfect therapist. Just give it some time <3 miss u

She looks up from her phone to see two children run to the turtle, laughing. They place their hands on its shell, patting it lightly at first. They discover the shell is hard, then slap with all their strength. More children surround the turtle—five more children, seven. To the side, a tall white man in a Hawaiian shirt shouts.

"Alright, kids, play nice with the turtle," he says.

All the children hop on the turtle's back, some spilling off from lack of room but hopping back on again. The turtle walks slower, then stops. "Why'd you stop? You dumb turtle!" Another suggests hitting its back because that's how her dad starts their car. The kids wallop the turtle's shell, and Turtledove hops off the rocks.

"Stop doing that!" Tiny fists keep swinging. A native lifeguard sprints toward the turtle, beating Turtledove to the scene and shoos the kids away with a booming "off!" The children scatter. A small yet defined crack appears on its shell—fresh, he notes. The white man asks what the problem is, and the native explains.

"Oh, sorry, I didn't know," and gathers the children and walks away.

"Hūpō," the native says under his breath. Turtledove apologizes for the native having to police the land from white people. The native gives her an "uh huh," and tends to the damage.

The conference room is half-full and calm, but Turtledove's microphone is cutting in and out. As a tech tries to fix it, more folk funnel into the room, academics from all walks of life ready to talk about unity and community and honoring the colonized. A Chicano comes into the room wearing a beige Pendleton, boot-cut blue jeans with a Mexican flag bandana sticking out of his butt pocket, and a red MAGA hat. He sits near the front row so the panelists can't miss him. The panelists all lean into each other while looking at the man, laughing at him, calling him "pendejo" and "cabrón," saying he needs an education. Turtledove can barely concentrate with her phone face up next to the broken microphone, service still unavailable. Suddenly people line the room and make it claustrophobic.

The MAGA Chicano stares at Turtledove like a crook, but she avoids his eyes, watches her lifeless phone instead. The bars replenish. She hears her chosen name.

"Turtledove," a panelist says. The whole room stares. She smiles, straightens the black denim vest, fixes her posture.

"Thank you, ASA, first of all, for allowing our truths to be expressed with like-minded academics and marginalized brothers and sisters." A smattering of applause eats up the silence. Turtledove's phone lights up, a new text from Moose.

"Before we begin, I want to acknowledge that we present today's discussion within white architecture built atop stolen ground. Specifically, the indigenous . . . "

"So what?"

The MAGA Chicano laughs in his chair with a leg victoriously folded over his knee. The panelists tell him to be quiet, be respectful.

"I just want to know—so what if this land is stolen?" MAGA Chicano asks. "What are any of you going to do about it? Pat your own backs about being smarter than your parents? Y'all don't do nothing but talk!"

Panelists continue to argue with the MAGA Chicano as the audience gets restless. They call him "hate monger," "racist," "pocho," "pendejo" again, "cabrón" again; everything academics are taught to chop down colonizers by the knees.

"You don't know me, putas," he says, proudly from his seat. "My family come from the Zapotec people of Oaxaca. Now what you gotta say? The chica talkin' that bullshit about 'stolen land' probably has a family full of settlers. You think that big-ass Mexican flag on her pinche metalhead vest makes her some innocent, victimized Chicana? Mija, you're a thief. All of you are. Especially all you fake-ass gabachos clapping over her pretty words. None of y'all do shit else to help colored folk besides say 'people of color' when you really wanna say 'nigger,' or 'spic.' At least the 'racists' y'all talk shit about aren't afraid to accept America as it is now: better, cleaner, and run by men with real plans."

The man goes on and on as the panelists yell just as loud. Some audience members are unable to withstand the awkward air and start leaving. Turtledove wants to shut him down. She wants to spit back everything she learned from her doctorate to wire his mouth shut, she wants to scream with the gale force necessary to knock his stupid hat off his head. But looking around, Turtledove sees only arguments, hears them dissolve into feedback. Among the chaos, she checks her phone. Messages trapped in limbo hours earlier have finally gone through—the pictures, the texts, the poem—and Moose answered.

stop

swim

To
    the Earth
    my blood

fixed it for ya. Now with 50% less cheese.
Miss you, too. Plz be safe?

"She's not even paying attention," MAGA Chicano says, pulling Turtledove away from Moose's text. "Y'all pretend to care about the ancestors and the lands until you're hit with too much truth. Now what ya gotta say?"

The other panelists call for security. Turtledove puts her phone back down by the broken microphone and leaves it there. She stands up, the creak in her chair broadcasts a signal. She steps down to start walking toward the exit. MAGA Chicano sits in a chair she'll have to walk past to leave. She sees his mouth ready to bark.

She runs. In her dash, her hands leave the comfort of her black denim pockets and fasten over the MAGA hat. She is a blur leaving the conference room. MAGA Chicano's footsteps can't catch up to her now that she's kicked off her heels. The echoes of "come back here," and "pinche puta," bounce off the hallway walls.

Outside, she's lost him, but she can't stop. Her legs drive her to rocks and water. Sand flies into the air as she now sprints, brief clouds created by panic. At the tide line, she stops to throw the hat into the ocean—a canvas of perfect blue now blemished by a red dot.

Turtledove looks at the new stain created in the water. She wants it to drown. As she starts to leave, she can't help but think of the earth's stomach, how it already aches with tires and trash and lost boats and lost lives. All she ever offered for remedy was an acknowledgment from an ivory tower that the earth exists, is sick, and woe is it. She walks away from podiums saving no Native lives, walks away using their graves as a path back to her offices; the Tongva still don't have their land back no matter how many times she reminds an audience that the Tongva still don't have their land back. She fed the earth a poisoned hat and called it a victory.

Here is new medicine: her shoulders push her into the ocean to undo the pollution. The hat was swiftly carried far into the blue, the tide growing animalistic with its waves. Nevertheless, she pours herself into the water, paddling with the strength she did not have when her Palestinian colleague was fighting her own battle. One wave hits Turtledove like a fist, and she somersaults under water while trying to regain her composure. The black denim vest loosens from her body, drowning in the waves out of reach of her hands. The MAGA hat falls back into her possession, while the black vest sinks further into the ocean: the pins, patches, stitching, ink, buttons, all return to a life underneath the earth. With her head out of water, she sees the turtle; shell repaired by Native islanders, scars dwarfed by the parts that remained whole despite the violence. It crawls on its own power along the beach, basking in solitude as Turtledove swims back to shore.

Waiting for Mo'

Mo',

You live in a red state, but I write this waiting for you to meet me for lunch on your visit back to Los Angeles. I sit on the blue bench directly across the street from Pizzamania, watching the last of its customers trickle in and out. The store announced it was going out of business months ago, the rumor mill saying it's already been leased by some white punks to be turned into another pizza place named The End of the World. You were busy with your big boy job in Michigan and couldn't come back to California until the store, as you and I knew it, was on its last legs. Sorry if that comes off as hostile—I am excited to see you. I am excited to hear your voice straight from your mouth instead of through a cell phone; to talk each other's ears off until the store closes for the last time, to eat one last large pineapple and shrimp pizza. I am also excited to hear your misery. Let me explain:

The house you and your fiancée bought looks over a hill in Kalamazoo. It fed your excitement to see wildlife and stars, to sit outside and watch fireflies the way *city living* never allowed. A cheap price sandwiched you between two old white families whose houses sported *TRUMP/PENCE* signs in their grass like weeds. They said, "You two are the *good* kind of Muslims!" as though planting a gold star on your and your Hindi fiancée's chests. They flaunted their open carry privileges around you, saying things about being a good guy with a gun, triple checking that you weren't the bad guy. They spoke slowly around you despite Urdu being your distant second language. In our phone calls, you mentioned selling the house eventually, hoping to make your way back to Los Angeles if better jobs opened up. I hoped to use your melancholy today to pull you back here, to prove that you and your fiancée are safer here than in a red state.

As if you never had problems in Los Angeles. Maybe you've forgotten your undergrad cohort who believed they could use your background as fodder for terrorism jokes. In exchange, your mostly Asian circles told you it was OK to make jokes about their background, their names, their faces. You never obliged, instead you took shots at their hand-me-down Hyundais because, as you say, cars are your real identity. Still, I am banking on you forgetting our second to last trip to Pizzamania when we got drunk off Irish car bombs and sour cocktails at the bar near campus before stumbling over to our shrimp and pineapple.

We sobered up at the parking lot in your car, a Honda S2000 which you loved like a child. Every penny at your—your words—*garbage bank teller gig* went into the gloss of that convertible. You opted to live at home for a few extra years no matter how much you complained about the stringent traditions of your Pakistani household, your staunchly religious siblings, their hatred of your Indian fiancée. No one used the house's garage but you; as escape, you spent hours working on the S2000, serenaded by the sounds of wrenches and a warm engine. I know nothing about cars, but my memory is a steel trap: I don't forget the things people love.

For example, you love "Purple Rain" by Prince, and I pray you won't remember how I shamed you while we sobered up the last time I saw you.

"You can't think of a better Prince song to like other than *the* poser song?"

"It's a great song!"

"True, but *everyone* thinks it's a great song. It's too easy."

"Why is easy bad?"

"It's just lame when an artist's poser song is your favorite song, dude. It shows you don't give their other music a chance. You can't just listen to what the radio tells you to listen to, man! Can't you think for yourself?" and this all sounded contentious and petty and I'm sorry.

You never loved music the way I do, just as I never thought of cars as more than scrap metal. You would never call me by my punk name, instead always using my real name, [   ]. You never understood punk, never *wanted* to understand punk, but you let me love it. I wanted to do the same for you, but I couldn't.

"I just like the way it sounds, man. I'm a sucker for pretty love songs."

"But it's about the end of the world. In the apocalypse, blue and red skies make purple."

You probably don't remember me saying that, or how I clearly felt better than you for preferring "Erotic City" or "Black Sweat," because a rogue Slurpee collided with your S2000's windshield, painting the glass in Wild Cherry slush. Two white boys walked past the car flipping us off. They screamed, "Je suis Charlie, you terrorist motherfuckers!"

I wanted to get out of the car and fight, but you told me to stay, assured me you had been through worse. It made me want to fight the fucking world. But those were the words that comforted you—*I've been through worse.* The two white boys disappeared into the dark, and I calmed down. We cleaned the red sugar from your car and laughed away the profiling.

"To be fair, your passport makes you look Iranian," you said.

My joke has always been that I am a double minority, cursed to be Black and Latino at the same time; when I get pulled over, I risk being beaten by a billy club before deported to the wrong Latin American country.

Ha.

We were both twelve when the Twin Towers fell; both old enough to know targets had temporarily been removed from every colored back except for Arabs. My parents hung the American flag from their cars like shields, despite being afraid of it—whose blood do you think colors those stripes, you know? But they felt protected in ways you felt afraid, and I don't need to tell you about your own fears, my friend.

When we met, I was afraid of you. We signed up for a summer class abroad in London. I made it to the airport before you and met the other students on the trip. White girls. Everywhere. They saw a vacation inside a blowoff class: comparative literature in theater arts. A few blondes made fast friends singing Katy Perry's "California Girls," then stopped when I walked up to find a seat. That day, I wore a small 'fro, a backpack, torn jeans, a leather jacket, and a ~~Germs t-shirt~~—sorry, *a* band T-shirt. The blondes looked afraid, side-eyed me as I came closer to our gate, hastily moved their bags away from where I sat. I never told you that.

I never told you about my jealousy. The blondes were more receptive when you walked toward the gate wearing clean jeans, a nice haircut, and an *OBEY* T-shirt. They even opened up a seat for you and your bags. I never told you I already knew your name was Mohammad before you introduced yourself, saying *but my friends call me Mo'*. The itinerary provided to us prior to the trip listed all the student names: I saw yours and froze, found solace joking with my cousin, who—to this day—still sports American flags on the side of her mom-van that cover her son's face like an umbrella.

"There's a Mohammad on my flight, cuz!"

"Dios! Be careful! Try to get an aisle seat so you can trip him if he tries anything."

Mo', I am so sorry. If it means anything, you, and X, and Bōkun are the only faces that have stayed with me. The blondes are faceless.

X, as you do know, was the first person I met on the trip. The light reflecting off her septum piercing caught my attention at first. Her chestnut hair offset her whiteness among the other blondes, and her flannel made me wonder if we could talk about Nirvana for the entire twelve-hour flight. We did not. Nonetheless, she looked at me without cowering like the other students. Of course, I fell in love. You felt the same for Bōkun. The lie is you noticed her straight, raven hair among the blondes; how she read quietly in a corner seat while the other white girls sang obnoxiously loud; how her monochrome clothes made you feel an ease that everyone else's bright colors did not. Truth is Bōkun was the only Japanese student in our group—of course we both noticed her immediately.

You told me how you braced for a conversation with her in broken English, how you prepared to speak slow and listen intently to piece together her attempted syllables. You were surprised when she sounded eloquently American. She told you about her mono-lingualism, how she went by Amanda throughout middle school and high school to avoid people mispronouncing her name, but demanded people call her Bōkun in college. You loved her name, how she stopped accommodating when she entered college. You always wanted that kind of bravery, the unapologetic celebration of your name. Still, you introduced yourself to me as, *my friends call me Mo'*, knowing most of your friends were not Pakistani or Arab or even Muslim.

"It makes ordering Starbucks easier!" This was also your joke.

Neither of us knew we were rooming together until we got to the flat itself. We got the beds we wanted, sides of the closet we wanted, portioned off the fridge so we wouldn't eat each other's food, and talked about *The Simpsons* until we finished unpacking. As soon as the last shirt wrapped around a clothes hanger, our cohort went out for our first night outing.

All of us walked to some nightclub close to the flats. X and the blondes guzzled collective gallons of mixed drinks while dancing on the hallway sized dancefloor, celebrating being 19 and legally drunk. You and I stood with Bōkun and a few others. We were all twenty-one at the time, so the gloss of drinking did not glisten quite as well.

The PA poured out American pop, stuff I know you dug. I caught you bobbing your head arrhythmically as the whites gyrated. Even still, I remember our first big laugh as a group when Katy Perry's music entered the room and the white girls yelled CALIFORNIA GIRLS despite the song actually being called "Firework" or some shit.

"Alright, let's pretend we don't know them, get one more drink, and sneak out. Maybe they won't find their way back," you said. We loved being wallflowers. We made more jokes at the expense of the whites, but eventually, our corner started dancing too. You still tell me seeing Bōkun trying to do the shuffle was one of your favorite moments of the trip. You caught me stealing glances at X, wondering how nice it would be to move to her movements.

The fourth night of the trip, I wanted to go to a punk show. You and Bōkun wanted to get away from the blondes, and X tagged along because she claimed she loved all music. The Tube didn't go all the way to Hackney, so we walked a mile through streets less pristine—the graffiti reminded us of Los Angeles, as did the homeless asking for spare quid. You happily gave a few coins here and there, while Bōkun and I had nothing to give that we hadn't saved exclusively for the show and a bus ride home. X, as you pointed out long after we returned to America, kept her eyes lost to the scenery and her purse clutched to her chest. She only stopped squirming when we reached The Macbeth.

The line outside flooded the sidewalk with leather jackets and beards. The four of us stood together for about a half an hour waiting for doors to open, talking about home and how much we didn't miss it. X lost herself in the wonder of living on unfamiliar soil, how she eventually wanted to move to London. She talked about her love of traveling, how she spent summers in Hawaii with her family, had vacationed in Italy a couple of times, how she couldn't wait to visit *some Asian country* the following year. You didn't see Bōkun's face, the grimace. Instead, you politely said how long it took you to save up for this trip, how the endless work hours between school rarely allowed for extended vacations. You and Bōkun shared a wish to spend more time in nature. Your elders found sanctuary in cities, felt moving anywhere else risked a death sentence. That didn't keep you from dreaming about going to bed in nature, to listen to the streets and hear ghosts walk over the gravel rather than the vitriol of traffic. I could see a quiet jealousy infect your smile when Bōkun told us about a camping trip near Yosemite, how she escaped people for a weekend to sleep under the stars; how she slept on grass among a soundtrack of gentle river water as fireflies danced above her face.

We both said, "Damn, I wanna see fireflies!" and owed each other cokes.

Later, years, you would tell me how annoyed you were with X when she interrupted Bōkun's story to tell us about her own family's semi-annual camping trips, that she saw fireflies at the rate people watched movies. The line started moving inside the venue just before you could say, ~~must be nice to afford to be anywhere, anytime, with no problem, white girl!~~ anything.

Inside, we all stood next to the bar and spent too many pounds on pints, getting drunk before the first band even started. You give me shit all the time about how great my memory is, but I can't remember anything about the bands that night. Honestly, I try to forget. You saw me drunkenly hop into mosh pits like it was my turn at double-dutch, ramming into English punks as sweat drenched my smile. The three of you avoided the chaos. Bōkun tried to nod her head to the rhythm, but she could never find it among the distorted echoes. One of the bands was too avant-garde even for me: seven white boys with one member wearing a giant football helmet and another member banging on the helmet with a mallet like it was a xylophone. The singer hopped off stage at one point and screamed directly in people's faces, including yours.

WHAT TURNS!

YOU ON!

WHAT TURNS!

YOU ON!

WHAT TURNS!

YOU ON!

Some audience members were receptive, pointing to the singer and screaming, "you, mate!" You tried to be so nice as his spit caked your glasses on TURNS! and his breath painted your lenses with steam on ON! You smiled and smiled and smiled. You didn't have to.

We all kept drinking as the bands kept on, your backs eventually loosened from the wall, but you didn't dare go into the pit—I don't blame you. The punks got too rowdy for me, swinging fists instead of hips, with a fight breaking out in the middle of the dance floor being our cue to leave. I remember all of us staggering out of the venue, pointing at street art glazed over the walls on Hackneys' streets. I held an arm over X's shoulders as she pointed toward different pieces on the wall and said, "That one's a Banksy, right? That one's totally a Banksy!"

You and Bōkun walked ahead of us, your legs just as noodled but at a further distance from one another. I asked you once what you had talked about while X called everything a Banksy (even some fucking tree), and you said *art*.

You said, "Bōkun told me that the art in that city reminded her of Yayoi Kusama. She's apparently someone who needs to make art, needs to name her own creations, needs to express who she is and how she felt on the inside, otherwise she'd kill herself. It was kinda cool. While you and X drunk-flirted behind us, we looked at the walls and saw the art of a bunch of souls who were saved for at least one more day. Bōkun said it reminded her of how precious the little things were. I swear to God, the colors got brighter."

Mo', honestly, I don't even remember the paintings on the brick. I barely remember how you helped us onto a double-decker bus when we were all too drunk to walk the rest of the way back to the flats. I was upset you weren't as drunk as the rest of us, that you aided me and X to a seat like we needed canes. At a stop, we saw some white punks from the show loitering. Moments before our bus pulled up, they jumped a Sikh man in a business suit. The Sikh man didn't stand a chance, never tried to swing back, gave himself to the thrashing in hopes the white punks would leave him be sooner. They walloped him, tore his business attire and riffled through his briefcase. Despite taking everything from the Sikh man, the white

punks kept thrashing and thrashing and thrashing. Through the gasps and shrieks, I pretended not to hear one of them sing,
WHAT TURNS!
YOU ON!
WHAT TURNS!
YOU ON!
WHAT TURNS!
YOU ON!
You couldn't stop staring at the violence, even as the bus drove away. The rest of us forgot how to talk, forgot to place our hands on your shoulders. We rode back in complete silence, sobriety trying to take a seat with us. The streetlights danced to the chorus of the night, the rhythm of my blurred vision. I hoped you would turn away from the window, even for a second, to enjoy the music with me; hoped you would turn away from the brown mirror beaten and alone. The lights could have been the fireflies you wanted. Instead, we returned and said nothing about the streets. I asked to borrow the bedroom so I could help X sober up, and you happily took the couch ~~while X and I fucked on your bed I'm so sorry~~ while her and I slept.

When we returned to America, we all made a dumb *happy-ending* promise to stay in touch. X and I continued to date, and I do thank you again for your tolerance of her outside of vacation. I thank you for not laughing at her grimaces as she lied about enjoying pineapple and shrimp pizza with us. Thank you for pretending to like her, especially at her parties with her other white friends, how she aggressively tried to set you up with her brown friends.

I apologize. Should have warned you. Two years after we came back from England, I had dinner at her parents' mansion. George Zimmerman had just been acquitted for murdering Trayvon Martin. I fumed to X for nearly an hour while we sat in her bedroom waiting for dinner—pot roast, tasteless potatoes, some sort of beet, other white shenanigans—and she stared at her childhood stuffed animals as I yelled. The version I told you was that she nodded politely and let me vent. Then dinner came around and her parents applauded the decision, happy that someone trying to keep his neighborhood safe from thugs earned his freedom. I told you she fought them, but that wasn't true. She doubled down on what her parents said and pointed at me as a prime example of a well-behaved minority. "Such a polite young man compared to these gangsters," she told them. I didn't say a word as I ate their tasteless potatoes.

I should have told you the day before our two-year reunion camping trip, when you and I had a sober meal at Pizzamania during Ramadan. I apologize for thinking fasting was easy; for saying Islam was the best religion because whites could never adapt to the discipline. You clearly saw my desire to fast with you for one day as a way to temper the guilt I'll always have for having been afraid of you. "I feel like you're just trying to piss off X's Protestant parents," you said, "but I appreciate you."

That morning I had eaten two eggs and toast, then drank nearly a half-gallon of water before napping throughout the day to expediate the fast, per your recommendation. You said I looked like a ghost walking into Pizzamania.

You laughed. We ate. I felt Cherry Coke crawl down my throat like water hitting desert dirt. The steel plate holding our entire pizza emptied sans thin strands of cheese and loosened pineapples to keep crumpled napkins company. At this point, I grew a larger 'fro while between degrees, and you had just gotten an engineering degree and grew out a full, victory beard. You weren't soured by the white frat guys staring at our hair while we ate, cringing when our laughter swelled. No. We prepped for the reunion trip and talked about escape.

Mo', I know you absolutely hated the reunion trip, and often point to it as the reason you couldn't live in California anymore, why you took the job in Michigan, so I won't ink anything about the trip itself. But I wanted to say you are not a poser. You are not obligated to like anything to prove you understand something. Had Bōkun made it to the reunion, she would have said the same thing.

The whole weekend, the blondes surrounded us, and you just needed to go home. You still tell me it's OK that X asked for us to hitch a ride with you in your S2000 to and from the trip, but still I think about our cramped bodies. How, on the way back, we left late when the freeways were pitch black, and one of your headlights burnt out thirty miles from any rest stop. X and I argued violently for most of the trip as we shared the passenger seat of your two-seater. I have mentioned many times how I wish you'd stop blaming yourself for this night, for trying to get us back home as fast as possible. It was still Ramadan, but you should have stopped for yourself when the sun went down. Instead, you let us bicker inches away from your ear as the hunger tugged at your eyelids. We should have shut up and given you water, but X and I were too distracted by our own vitriol to notice that you nodded off. Slowly, naturally, to the point X and I assumed it purposeful, your S2000 bled over several lanes and careened off the 5, down a steep hill. So sudden, we all fell in silence, forgetting to scream. The car bounced off rocks, all at once at the speed of light and molasses; like days going by slowly, years at a sprint. Suddenly, it was over, wounds now wide open. The metal beaten by jagged stones, the second headlight gone blind, and the windshield become fallen rain.

I know you hate this memory, too, but when the car stopped just short of a bigger drop, I became convinced we couldn't let this part of the weekend go. The three of us got out of the car, collectively clothed in minor cuts. We did what we were supposed to do in accidents—ask if we're all OK, cry, check the damages, cry some more. Your baby would be deemed totaled, but you walked away from the wreckage as soon as you realized no one died, then planted yourself at the edge. X and I took a break from anger to join you. Over the cliff, we saw a deep night; a canvas of stars washed over the Earth, trees dressed as silhouettes, animals sleeping with shadows as blankets. We couldn't see a goddamn thing.

Then you pointed at the sky—the dark blue tainted with rain clouds and the vivid glow of our annual California grapevine fires.

The purple made you laugh into the gorge, tears rolling into your mouth. Not an ounce of fear held on to your bones as you laughed into the chaos. The darkness hid X from view, but we heard her ask, "What are you laughing at, Mo'? This is so fucking scary. I feel like the world is ending."

"Good," you said.

Right now, I am still waiting for you to arrive so we can eat this pineapple and shrimp pizza like we used to. I am waiting to be reminded that you are alive, and that your red state neighbors hadn't beaten the Islam out of you. In the time I have written this, I have seen students from our old campus walk in and out, satiated, tinier than I remember. I expected a bigger crowd.

Whatever. More pizza for us, right? More space for me to show you how much room Los Angeles has for people like you and me. As I write this, I still want to save you from Midwestern exile, but now I am not even convinced I'm safe sitting on this blue bench alone. Now I am not convinced that you're safer with me white people who'd use you to feel less racist. Now I am not convinced you didn't already escape.

I haven't checked my phone since sitting down, as it has been on silent so I can be pleasantly surprised when you eventually show up. And, when you do, I want to be right about what happens next: When you move back, you'll bring your Hindi fiancée and find a better engineering job near the ocean. We'll find Bōkun and invite her and her husband out for drinks, and you will all meet my wife. We will all look like a painting; every color expressed with the vibrance of lights, the snapshots of euphoria we lost back in London.

I want to be right, but the only thing I'm certain of is that I *want* to be right.

Love,
[   ]

[   ],

Sorry I missed our lunch, but I am back in Michigan.

There's no blue in the sky tonight.

Just reds from flames that are too close to us.

But the fireflies are out.

Their bodies breach the night with bright lights that dim the burning crosses over the hill.

I think you would like them.

—Mo'

The Good Hair

Pops did not teach me to have good hair. I learned by mistake. A section of unwashed afro knotted into a small dreadlock in the back of my head, and he told me to cut it off. Pops did not like the growth, did not like the curls. Pops' afros have long since been taken by razors. Always said he preferred Mamá's hair seduced by straighteners that fried her waves over decades. But, even when I questioned the body they gave me, I loved the hair.

When I left home, I turned the afro into dreadlocks—hair that forced me to be gentle with myself. Now I keep my scalp washed so the roots don't dry out, can grow without pain. I slow down to navigate the right shampoos so sulfates don't eat the locks. I can walk into Black salons and not be scared off by everything Pops never taught me, can navigate tender-headedness and peppermint. Don't have to code-switch if I don't wish, no need of proof of the southern Black family from which my Pops was raised. They accept the femineity Mamá gifted me. They take water and wax, sometimes crotchets, and keep the dreadlocks thriving. My hair is safe in Black femme hands, nurtured into onyx. I learn time. I learn how to enter the world. I learn when the new growth breathes from my roots, to palm roll it into who I want to be. Twists tightened by Africa, wound into rope fastened to climb into Pops' sun.

* * *

Moose never saw Pops beaten by the cops, but he knows how it happened blow for blow. Pops forgot his wallet on the way to Alameda to meet his dealer and Pops raced back home so neither Mamá nor Moose could catch him slipping. A cop pulled him over on Firestone Blvd near Moose's high school for going 62 in a 35. Both cars pulled up behind an SUV full of people waiting on a tow truck, all of them on cell phones either calling AAA or killing time on social media. The cop did not believe Pops when he said he was Unk's brother, especially without an ID. The cop, porcelain statue of the devil, called Pops a liar. No way he could be related to such an upstanding Black man. Pops knew he should not have gotten loud, but Pops got loud. His eyes wanted to scorch the cop. This was enough for Pops to be pulled out of the car and cuffed. Backup came. Two more cars. Pops got louder and louder. Cell phones from the SUV pointed at all the cops like guns. Behind the screens, the sounds of "Stop it! Stop it!" burst in the air. The other cops came to restrain Pops further, slamming him face first onto his car's hood, correcting his gesticulations with batons.

"My brother is one of you!" Pops said.

"Shut the fuck up, nigger."

A rogue baton collided with the back of Pops' neck. His body became an earthquake until his face collapsed. Before Unk asked if his brother was ok, he said, "I knew those rocks would get him in trouble. Been tellin' him to quit since I quit. Shit." Before Unk gave Pops his first hug out of the hospital, he lamented, "We lost a good officer. Had to fire him for whoopin' my brother, but that's what the courts said had to happen." Before Moose could say, "I love you, Pops," when he returned home from his broken bones, before Moose could beg, "No more drugs," he said, "I never want to see Unk or his kids again."

* * *

Punk does not celebrate ACAB; it mourns the idea. Moose carries ACAB on his clothes, a pin gifted from a musician friend as consolation for being unable to get Pipebomb! on the bill for a hybrid punk and drag show. They sold DIY merch, enamels that read things like, *Abolish I.C.E.*, *Death to 45*, *Fuck Gender*, and *ACAB*.

Moose wanted to give them cash for their work, but they insisted visibility from a friend like Moose was enough currency.

Pops' family, on the other hand, found currency in protection. They all wanted to be protectors. They wanted it more than being known as "family." Pops works security at a high-class nightclub in Los Angeles for a security agency run by Auntie. Unk had been a sheriff for thirty years before he retired, and most of his kids followed in his footsteps as beat cops. One of Unk's kids did not become a cop, instead moving away to Texas after turning eighteen, and working at a car factory. One daughter hated the cop life, quit, and sold auto-insurance. The other daughter basked in the lifestyle. She climbed the ranks swiftly, became proficient in combat, and made a record number of arrests in her first couple of years.

On video, Eric Garner is choked to death by NYPD officer Daniel Pantaleo. The officer loses his job, but no other indictments are served. Not long after, Moose's cop cousin gifts most of the family "Blue Lives Matter" flags as a reminder that she is a good cop, that she puts her life on the line for the safety of every single one of them.

* * *

I burned the flag cousin BlueLives gave me. Set it on fire at a Pipebomb! show when we ended our set with our one ACAB song everyone knows. Obviously, I never told BlueLives. In shared spaces, we refuse to talk anyway. Only fake smiles, then move on.

We practice this ritual after Pops and Mamá convince my wife and I to visit the cousins on the Fourth of July for a potluck barbeque. Driving to the cousin's house, I keep my hands firm on the wheel, plainly visible to onlookers. My wife, Turtledove, cradles a bowl of gallo pinto on her lap, holds a plate of taquitos by her feet. This will be the first meal we'll all have together since before the protests downtown in our war against cops. We wear everyday outfits: Turtledove sports a nice turquoise summer dress with her natural curls flowing over her shoulders; my sunglasses are big enough to cover a welt over my left eye not yet healed. On my chest pocket, an enamel pin with the letters *ACAB*, its blood red shade a spotlight.

The cousins rarely have anything to talk about with me. They don't care that I am in a punk band, and don't understand why I want to "do more school" by becoming a college professor. But it makes Pops happy to see us spend time with his side of the blood.

The house is in an affluent neighborhood in Los Angeles, where my cousin's lawn alone sprawls the entire square footing of my parent's apartment. Still, the house is the smallest on the street. A ton of family have come from Texas and Louisiana, many of whom I have not seen since I was a child. They all recite the same script: call me by my birth name, followed by, "Is that you?" then a choice of, "Chile I ain't seen you since you was up to my knee," or, "Where you get all that hair from? I know you didn't get it from yo' pops' bald ass." When Auntie is in the room, she tells them, "He goes by Moose now. All that heavy metal and protestin' he be doin'."

"You doin' security like your Pops?" a few ask.

"No," I say. "I'm a college professor."

"Bet that don't pay one damn bill."

Every interaction the same: I smile, I nod, I wait for their "nice to see you again," that they sometimes follow with a sardonic, 'Moose.' Turtledove and Mamá hang out on a couch, flanked by a few other mixed relatives. Pops and Unk both married Latinas, so a quarter of the house is filled with Afrolatinx cousins. This is made most obvious by the potluck.

The kitchen hosts a long table decorated with defiantly Black and brown food. Mamá brought Costa Rican tamales to dwarf the Mexican ones. Others brought collard greens, baked mac and cheese, corn bread, and BBQ ribs. Pops brought store-bought fried chicken to accidentally offset Auntie's homemade version. A pot of gumbo simmers on the stove next to another pot of red rice. Hot dogs and burgers lay over flames on a grill outside, and American flags litter the grass. Red, white, and blue streamers hang from the roof, and a pile of store-bought fireworks keep warm on the patio for the night's festivities.

We plan to leave before the fireworks go off. I have never enjoyed the spectacle, never understood the need to set fire to the sky to show an appreciation for a country. As a child in Southeast LA, I heard explosions throughout June and July—exuberant neighbors who got hold of some roman candles and M-80s. I could never tell the difference between the fireworks and gunshots. Pops blamed gangs in the area; Mamá worried about cops' trigger fingers. Regardless, Mamá always asked me to just *hope* for fireworks when I heard explosions.

One afternoon, a barrage of noise infested the streets. Machine gun or a line of firecrackers, I can't say. Did not stop for thirty minutes. I buried my head under the covers of my bed to dull the noise, fear swapped for annoyance. Every pop accompanied police sirens near and far. The dissonance nearly drowned me until it didn't. The noise became numbing, and over time I stopped fearing explosions. I miss the panic. I miss being naïve.

Dinner time at BlueLives's house means grabbing our own plate and gorging on bits of everything. The men get their food first and return to the living room to watch whatever sport they're betting on. Women and children go second, and I wait to grab table scraps so I can avoid the most people. There is plenty of food when I get there, but BlueLives stands in the kitchen talking to another family member I have not seen in some time. I don't remember her name.

"Let me get a good look at you," Relative says, touching my dreads. She says I have hair like another relative I don't remember. "But these look nice cause you got that good hair from both your mama and your daddy."

Comments about how fast I have grown come and go, and she compliments my floral shirt. The relative wears a long purple Sunday dress, as though she were on her way to or from church. BlueLives' plainclothes are blue jeans and a red plaid. She avoids my eye contact. Relative notices a pin on my jacket among many and asks what it means. I see BlueLives brace for the answer. She knows what *ACAB* means.

"It's just a punk rock thing," I say.

"Guess I'm not part of the club," she laughs.

BlueLives and I fake giggles. BlueLives's smirk is not as overexaggerated as my doubled over laughter. From that angle, my relative notices the welt over my left eye.

"What happened to your face, chile?" she asks.

"Cops," I say.

BlueLives grabs her plate of food, gives our relative a kiss on the cheek, and walks to the sports room with the other men. In there, folks crowd around a television eating food off TV trays. Pops and Unk sit next to each other on the couch and argue over their teams, BlueLives' Blue Lives flag is strung up on the wall behind them. I overhear BlueLives yell at her husband about taking up too much room on one of the couches, then shouts erupt as a team scores some point. The sudden noise makes my eye welt throb.

It is an hour after dinner, so Turtledove and I decide to go home. We make our rounds saying goodbyes, hugging familials and strangers alike. I give BlueLives the politest nod I can muster. Pops is extra thankful we made it out to the cousin's house at all. Said it made it feel like normal times, before all the fussing. Pops holds his breath to stave off crying, his eyes transform into moist maroon orbs. He fights it, says, "Yo, those taquitos your girl made were jammin'!"

"Nigga, who says 'jammin'?" BlueLives said, eavesdropping as she gave Turtledove a half-hug goodbye. Pops cringes when Blue-Lives speaks, unable to ever contain his hatred toward the slur, no matter how retrieved by the culture. Nonetheless, they embrace, too. No harm dealt.

We take our Tupperware, make it into the car, then fasten seatbelts. Just before starting the engine, Turtledove tries to tell me she had a nice time, that all the food was delicious. My hands shake on the steering wheel. A police van worms in and out of the street; it drives past us slowly. The driver stares into our car until his neck stops turning. The sky blurs into an opaque film as my breaths deepen. Turtledove wipes my eyes dry, pulls me into her chest. The seatbelt keeps me tied to the seat. Rather than unbuckle, she moves closer. Her chest staggers with mine.

She palms my left eye like a healer.

* * *

The other kids say Turtledove's hair is too black. "Eres tú negrita?"

No. She straightens her hair until she looks like her Chicana heroes.

After punk, after becoming "Turtledove," the degrees and degrees and degrees, she abandoned relaxers. She washed her hair. The water molding straight locks into coils. Brown fingers run through raven strands; every strand touched like a lover. Her feet soak in shampoo residue that pries dirt and the unwanted hand-prints of "can I touch your hair" from her follicles.

Oils, vinegars, rosewater.

Curls bounce like the sun jumping into the sky at dawn.

She learns how to wrap it in silk before sleep. Watches how Black women take care of their hair in YouTube videos. Turtledove has trouble with the pineapple wrap. She tries once, twice, their way isn't working for her but she doesn't want to correct them, three times, the wrap keeps coming undone, four times, is she letting these Black women down, five times, isn't she supposed to be the ally, six times. Seven times in the mirror. Tears held back "Eres tú negrita?" Tears cleanse. Hurt.

Eight times. She sleeps.

* * *

I am five, crying inside a Black-owned barbershop in Compton, the only one Pops trusts. The barber cape hangs from my neck. Pops requests a line shaved above my forehead to keep up with Black fashion. Meanwhile, Pops laughs with other Black men. I hear thunder in their bellies. I want to know how to laugh with the Black men.

I laugh with Pops when I am thirteen. We watch Ice Cube and Cedric the Entertainer play barbers in a Black neighborhood. I sport a small afro that Pops despises. Nonetheless, the film feels familiar; it is natural to laugh when Pops laughs. Pops' belly becomes a storm, loudest when Cedric the Entertainer says, "There are three things that Black people need to tell the truth about. Number one: Rodney King should've gotten his ass beat for being drunk in a Hyundai in a white part of Los Angeles. Number two: O. J. did it! And number three: Rosa Parks didn't do nuthin' but sit her Black ass down!" I laugh with Pops as the lights rise in the theater.

★ ★ ★

You, with stubby fingers that tap my shoulders at the Palladium in Los Angeles as we all waited for Jawbreaker. A gold waterfall of hair fell onto your shoulders, straight silk dyed a White American gloss. Your goatee peppered with age to let everyone know you know things. You singled me out for having dreadlocks and a high yellow complexion. You swayed drunk and snapped to the tune of Counting Crows' *A long December and there's reason to believe maybe this year will be better than the last.* The other white punks laughed. To you, dreadlocks belonged to singer Adam Duritz at the peak of mid-'90s fashion. To you, dreadlocks were another thing whites could smuggle from Africa and wear as a crown in front of cameras, tell the suburban kids, "We can have this, too! This that good hair!"

Me, with "Go fuck yourself" choked in my throat as I stood in the pit outnumbered. I had no witnesses. How much riper the space was for your body than mine, I get it. Jawbreaker played a blistering set of '90s aggression that you must have known (better) in your own youth. The whirlpool started; the sweltered bodies moved in unison in the mosh pit. "Boxcar" boomed, *You're not punk, and I'm telling everyone.* I lodged a right elbow into the small of your rusted back, then twists from both our bodies led my right elbow to strike your gray beard, *you don't know what I'm all about.* Call it an accident. You fell. No one picked you up. *I'm coloring outside your guidelines.* Feet in the slam dance painted you into the floor. I never saw you again.

1, 2, 3, 4, who's punk? What's the score?

* * *

This is a mosh pit. I am wearing my favorite At the Drive-In T-shirt: black threading, red and yellow design of a trojan horse with the word *¡Atención!* Now I stand in Downtown Los Angeles. My mouth is wrapped in a black bandana. The sun catches thousands in the eye, but we keep marching with signs demanding justice for Black life, full names recognized and scrawled on poster boards, shouted into Los Angeles smog.

Turtledove holds a megaphone, shouts battle cries mobilizing surrounding demonstrators, dressed head to toe in black. Pipebomb! flank me: bassist Duck wears a Mexican flag stitched onto his sleeve as he holds a sign that says, "Who do you call when the police murder?" and drummer Yacht stores away his whiteness underneath a "Black Lives Matter" sweatshirt as he holds a poster board saying, "How many <u>weren't</u> filmed?" All three of them speaking with anger after mine gave out. I look at the art spray-painted on walls that say the same things as our poster boards. The angry bodies swimming through the streets makes me feel as though the names gunned down by police live on beyond the portraits people carry.

Local businesses join the march, as do some students of mine, and some punk bands we know. Blaxican walks with my crew, a hoodie to keep warm and tennis shoes to make sure his feet don't give out before their time. He already earned his A before the marches even started.

In the distance, I hear *fuck.* playing a hardcore show at the steps of a government building. SkaterBoi using a megaphone as a mic, punks scrambling in circles to the music. We shove down the jealousy and vitriol for just one day. Ignore the advertisement guised as social justice. I want to hear his voice; I want to hear it in the ether of LA streets.

Now we kneel on Spring Street outside Los Angeles City Hall. The quiet washes over us like a prayer, a thousand heads lower to listen to speeches given. I listen to the names of other Black lives lost to police hands as cops surround us. The cops are gargoyles waiting for the sunset. Curfew is not until 6 p.m., and today's demonstration has been too peaceful to disrupt.

The gargoyles can't touch us.

We are going home for the day. We will be back tomorrow. It is only 4:13 p.m. An emergency alert sounds off on everyone's phones. Curfew has been pushed up to 4 p.m. We are all currently breaking the law. The gargoyles shake off their stone, push all of us off the streets. Turtledove, Pipebomb!, and I are safely inside Turtledove's SUV, trying to leave the vicinity. The gargoyles tackle protesters, replace poster boards with zip ties.

Blaxican is stationary, filming the assaults catching fire around him. I roll down my window to call out to him, to tell him to leave. Then a Black cop rushes Blaxican, points a gun directly at his eyes. The phone shatters when it reaches the pavement. Blaxican says, "Stop! Please! I didn't do anything!" I see the cop's familiar Black hands. I try to scream at Unk to leave my student alone, but a canister of teargas collides with Turtledove's windshield before my words can douse this fire. I am too slow to close the window. My eyes shut and burn.

* * *

214

Pops counts my fingers and toes when I am born to make sure I am whole.

* * *

Mamá's favorite story goes like this: "Remember the time you came home from preschool and you said, 'Mommy, mommy! Teacher said I'm Black, but I'm not. I'm peach, see!' and you pointed at your hand and even pulled out a crayon to prove it. It was so cute."

* * *

In the late '70s before white flight in South Gate, Mamá and Pops take solace in their white friends. Their friend group in high school could have been the Rainbow Coalition. Whites and browns and Blacks and whites and queers and whites. Pops' afro is a perfect black sphere, Mamá's hair is dyed red and swirls like Farrah Fawcett's. At age sixteen and seventeen respectively, their coalition approves of their race mixing. This is not Mamá's mamá who asked a priest, in Spanish, if Pops was the devil in black. This is not Pops' Thanksgiving when someone asked, "Who wants dark meat?" and Unk quickly blurts out, "Not [Pops]!" to uproarious laughter. Mamá and Pops' union has cured racism.

Decades later, now in their 50s, reuniting with their coalition through social media, Mamá and Pops watch their rainbow break— "MAKE AMERICA GREAT AGAIN" for banners, "ALL LIVES MATTER" for bios, "That's the couple we used to know! Takes me back to disco nights with you two, when life was so much better," in private messages. A video surfaces of Pops beaten by cops, the coalition commenting, "Shoulda listened to the officer and not yell like a maniac!" The coalition colored white and white and white and white and white and white.

* * *

215

Here is a phone. Payphone covered in graffiti in the late-'90s. It has a modest lean. Pops calls a woman who is not Mamá. Moose is with Pops, young and close to double digits. Moose hears, "Baby." Moose hears, "Rocks." Moose hears, "Don't tell your mother." The best way to stifle an argument is to pretend the words don't exist.

Later, decades, Pops works security at a nightclub to perfect the art of saving lives. He smiles gently at everyone: the celebrities who tip big, common folk who tip small, the customers who give him respect. He smiles when bullets fly past his ears after angry white clubbers sneak guns into the bar. He smiles ejecting a rich Persian man for inappropriately touching a female patron; the rich Persian man calls him a slur, then threatens a lawsuit. He smiles when one of his own pant legs tears wide open after breaking up fights between drunk trust fund babies.

He smiles at everyone in hopes his job does not disappear.

Moose is an adult with a master's in English. This must mean he knows all there is to know about words: how dangerous they are, how powerful, how sharp they can be when twisted in the wrong stomach. Moose hears his folks talk about Pops' job.

"I don't want to go into work on 'Fag Night' and get sick."

Moose wants to correct this before a queer friend is wounded, but Moose does not know how to correct this. Moose does not know if he needs to correct this—if he wants to correct this. Moose does not want to steal Pops' smile after working so hard to tattoo it where it belongs. Moose pretends the word does not exist.

"I don't want to go into work on '___ Night' and get sick."

With this context, who would?

"I don't want to go in on 'Baby Night' and get sick."

"I don't want to go in on 'Rock Night' and get sick."

"I don't want to go in on 'Don't tell your mother Night' and get sick."

Fair. Because what if this is the sickness:

Pops writhes on the bed. Vomit stains sheets Mamá refused to share for some time.

Pops drinks expired milk to prove to a young Moose it is still good.

Pukes into the kitchen sink; substances no longer numb his stomach.

And now Unk stands over Pops' bed like a wake, watching his brother disintegrate.

Unk says, "You're ruining your own life."

Unk is shocked Pops does not recover instantly after these words.

Unk tells a young Moose to stay out of the room while he fixes Pops.

Unk expects Moose will become a bastard at the rate Pops is going.

An older Moose would have said, "I am not you, Unk."

But young Moose wants to find the right words to help Pops wake up.

Young Moose does not want older Moose to say, "You're ruining your own life."

But Moose sees the blackness of Pops' baby afro stained with grays and whites.

Moose wants to tell Pops he does not want this hair.

I do not want baby. I do not want rock.

I do not want to tell my mother.

*　*　*

A motel in the projects. Nighttime. Pops walks downstairs to enter the maroon sedan Mamá is driving. German shepherds surround the car like sharks, but Pops shoos them away by name. The chocolate on his cheeks lost its color. Silence in the car weighs wheels down to a slow crawl home. I am eight years old and sit in the backseat, ask Pops for a video game. Mamá originally said, "No," gets mad because I ask again. Furiously yells the name they gave me at birth.

Now, I am a teenager in a puny Southeast LA house, playing video games with my bedroom door open. In my peripherals, Pops walks into the kitchen, puke crusted on his white T-shirt. His shoulder leans on a broken and elevated oven because his legs shake too much. I am old enough to not ask questions anymore. Pops stumbles into my room wearing only underwear. Pops grabs my guitar—a semi-functioning black and white Squier Stratocaster, a Christmas present from Mamá but signed from both parents—and strums mindlessly. Pops hums an Elvis tune, laughing. I am more afraid than ever that I don't understand Pop's laughter. Fear forces me to snatch the guitar back. We struggle for control until the guitar flies out of our hands and into my video games. The neck is broken, strings are cut, game disks shattered. Pops is still laughing.

Later, a year, Pops and Mamá and I watch *Ray* in theaters. Pops and Mamá and I watch Jamie Foxx portray music legend Ray Charles. Pops and Mamá and I watch this milestone in Black culture undercut by drugs. All the drugs. Jamie Foxx as Ray Charles convulses in a rehab bed, falls off a few times. A doctor turns on a light and Jamie Foxx as Ray Charles is scared. Nurses try to relax him, but he fights their arms away. Coughs brutalize his sleep, regurgitations choke his toilet. I have never seen this movie, but I know this scene blow for blow. Fiction, nonfiction, *based* on nonfiction. I just know, within my bones, this scene is true. Pops is immobile as he stares at the screen. Mamá is crying.

⋆ ⋆ ⋆

Here is another phone; modern, updated, keeps conversations clear in the late 2010s. Line #1 is Turtledove: Her glasses are pink, her black denim vest is punk. Her Mexican elders taught her to be afraid of the Blacks, "vijilando las lineas" when they came into the family stores, but she has undone those lessons by injecting other cultures into her lexicon. Her doctorate makes the wrong words appear as poison. She filters panels for a conference devoted to music, and flags one paper dedicated to dismantling patriarchal abuse of power in the music industry.

Line #2 is Moose: See his beard with sparse grays peppered into his face, the bottoms of his eyes are weighed down by years. Watch his dreadlocks fall over his face like a shamed hand.

Line #1—This girl has good ideas, but so much of her argument is anti-Black. First, she talks about Dr. Dre being misogynistic during the peak of gangster rap. Then there's stuff on R. Kelly and his abuses of underage females. It caps off with Bobby Brown's self-medication interfering with Whitney Houston's career. All *Black* men. Where are the white men that need to be dismantled? Freakin' white women, I swear!

Line #2—Whites are evil. Everyone knows that. It is a fucking joke at this point. But Dr. Dre did punch Dee Barnes for publishing a story that made him look bad. She's facing homelessness, while Dr. Dre is busy donating $70 million to private schools. And R. Kelly used his fame and power *like* a white dude, sleeping with the underaged without punishment.

Moose's line goes silent as Turtledove raises her voice. Mansplaining, belittling, making her feel unqualified to be an ally. Moose stews in his hatred of the phrase "self-medication." The words churning his stomach like disease, "As though crack can be prescribed by a doctor," he wants to say over Turtledove's distress. "He was a drug addict. She was a drug addict," he wants to say, disrupting Turtledove thoughts. "They ruined their own lives. I don't care if they're Black. Forgiving [us] for crimes of morality based on [our] culture's traumas corrects nothing," Moose wants to scream while he has invalidated Turtledove.

The punk sings, "They ruined their own lives."

Moose tries to erase words from Turtledove's tongue. "It caps off with Bobby Brown's self-_____ interfering with Whitney Houston's career." In the empty space of conversation, Moose hears, "baby," and "rocks," and "don't tell ____" and for the life of him he can't remember the last word of that sentence. Moose can't intellectualize this disharmony, so he apologizes to Turtledove while still wondering if he is who she was supposed to check the lines for. Moose is hidden behind his hair, Turtledove's curls bristle the receiver.

Line #2—I'm sorry, love. I'm just tired.

Line #1—So am I.

* * *

In the shower, my hair becomes anvils.
Wash the locks too often, they will break.
Wash the locks too little, strangers think there are bugs in the hair.
Water hits my feet like blast beats.
I hear the music.
Song from ancestors who want to fly, too.
I know the dance.
I want to dance.

* * *

But this is a slam dance. In downtown LA again, Turtledove screams slogans with every part of her throat now that a cop has confiscated her megaphone. Only Duck flanks me, wearing a Mexican flag around his neck as though it gave him the power to fly. Yacht was arrested ten minutes ago—he swatted a baton out of a cop's hand who was beating a Black femme protester, then he was awarded several boots to his ribs by the cop's back up. This is the sixth week of protests. The cops have killed at least ten more. Some fired, charged with nothing, and given a generous severance package. We still march to put them behind bars, to put them in the chair. But now the National Guard has taken the cops' place, and beat cops are armored with riot gear.

Local businesses have boarded up, and I begged students of mine—new and old—to stay home. I look at the graffiti defacing the art spray painted on walls. I see "White Power" and "All Lives Matter," spelled in white paint over "Black Lives Matter" and portraits of Black faces kept alive by local artists.

Now, as we kneel on Spring Street outside Los Angeles City Hall, my throat hiccups trying to say any name. We are surrounded by assault rifles, but we are all only armed with raised fists. In front of us, in the middle of the line of cops in riot gear at the top of City Hall's steps, cousin BlueLives stands with her baton fully extended, the padding on her vest and limbs secured and covering her Afrolatina skin. I see her face through the plastic face mask—she stares straight ahead into nothing as though we are all ghosts she refused to believe exist.

I stand up.

Turtledove begs me to stay on my knees.

I break from the group.

Walk toward the line of riot gear.

I walk slow to avoid rubber bullets for as long as I am allowed.

People are letting me pass as I try to disrupt BlueLive's blank stare with my presence.

I scream, "Cousin!"

I scream again, then I say her name. She looks at me, only moves her eyes. She grips the baton with more protective urgency than she would her own children. The black bandana around my mouth has slackened, so I rip it off my face for her to see. It floats to the ground. The other cops ready their batons. I say BlueLives' name over and over again. I hold my hands up as I climb City Hall's steps even though no guns have been drawn. BlueLives does not break her stare from mine. Now I am less than one foot away from her. I tower over her on a normal day, but I stand a couple of steps below her to meet her eyes.

"Cousin," I say. "What the fuck are we doing?"

I want her grip to loosen from the baton's neck, to shed the protective padding from her riot gear. But her eyes drift, fall on the *ACAB* pin still secured to my chest like Superman's "S." The enamel gleams pristine over red letters. BlueLives raises her baton higher than my hands. Becomes lightning that shatters my left eye.

I fall.

Each step fails to catch me as I fly over stone, my face kisses the concrete. I land on gravel at the bottom of City Hall. Blood mixes into my shirt, and now cop boots rush over me, covering my view of the sky like a murder of crows. Batons collide with protesters and become white noise. All I feel are feet on my body until Turtledove and Duck drag me away from the stampede. Flash bangs pockmark the sky, and I see different color smoke drown the floor. A rainbow promising a storm. The fire this time. No one warned me about fireworks igniting—how gorgeous explosions can be from the ground, how quiet the bursts so close to the face—so I count my fingers to make sure they are all there before I close my eyes. Everything goes black, but I can't wait to tell Pops I am still whole.

* * *

I am older than the age Pops was when I was born. We eat burgers with Mamá for Pops' 58th birthday. They even let me pay this time. When we eat, Pops says, "I hate the words 'African American.' I ain't from Africa. I'm from Hobbs, New Mexico. My momma's from Marshall, Texas. Ain't no one from Nigeria. Ain't no one that I know who was Black was a slave. Maybe 'cept my buddy Ron. Shit, my best friend from Hobbs growin' up. Used to be all messin' around town after school, ridin' bikes and playin' ball with our other friends. When we came to South Gate, me and Ron lost touch. Found out dude died not too long ago. Hadn't heard from him for years, then this happens. I cried, yeah. Who don't cry when your friend dies? I had a bunch of people die on me and cried every time. You can't help it. But I went to his funeral in Hobbs. Nothin' but white people. American flags everywhere. I was like, 'Yo, did Ron join the army or something?' but nah. Just became Republican. Loved Trump. Hated fags. I didn't get it. I coulda left. Didn't feel like I was seein' my friend anymore. Didn't even feel like I was supposed to be there with all them white people just starin' at me.

But the dude that rode bikes with me when I was a kid was in that box, still one of the only other Black people in that room—that wasn't gonna change. So, I stayed. Paid my respects. His white friends might have been uncomfortable with me standin' all next to them, but I didn't care. Let them be uncomfortable. They could celebrate their Trump Ron, but I celebrated the Ron I knew. That's all I needed. Them little American flags didn't do nothin' for me."

The In-N-Out bustles, but this table is an island. Mamá sits opposite me and Pops. Mamá looks at two men she feared she would lose, watches as we remain in her view. Pops approves of my dreadlocks now, tightened over years of letting my hair breathe Blackness, exhale Latinidad.

I look at Pops' smile—his teeth white and lips free from burns. Pops can hear, "Pops, could you not use that word. It's like the 'n-word' for queer folk," and say, "Ok, but I love ___ Night. They're nice people." Maybe that's enough, maybe it's not. But we can laugh. Mamá watches us exist then captures us. The camera makes certain we lean into one another forever, a torch lighting another torch. I hold a Double-Double, Pops throws up a peace sign with shades over his eyes. This joy frozen forever by a flashbulb.

Look at us both; existing. Still laughing.

* * *

Some years ago, on an afternoon plane from Portland that should have crashed, I met my wife Turtledove. In defiance of the elements and God, we landed. So, I invited her to a Pipebomb! show the following week in some dude's backyard in Southeast LA. A diverse show, the type we rarely got the chance to play for one reason or another—busy schedules, white hardcore bands love us more than marginalized bands, excuses excuses excuses. At this particular show, a couple of queercore bands and a punk act from Tijuana played with us.

I was so happy to play this show that I even invited my folks.

223

Of course, they declined, but "they sent their love" and hoped I "rocked out really hard." We set up just after dusk, the second band to play the show. The cops hadn't shown up yet, spirits still very high. The backyard burst with people—punks of all shapes and sizes, and some friends of mine who hated punk rock but still wanted to see me perform.

Mo' was in town with his fiancée. They both just arrived as we set up, both stood near the back where the fence held the backs of the older show-goers who wanted to chill and drink. Despite his brand-new style of a shaved head to counter his graying hair and sharpening widows peak, I spotted him immediately through the crowd. We happily cheers-ed from a distance when we made eye contact as I tuned my guitar—his Modelo Negro, my canteen of ice water. The pit itself held so many bodies I did not know, many of whom looked like me or Duck. But I spotted Lucy, freshly emancipated from matrimony if my last phone call with Munkey was any indication, in the pit talking with some folks I tangentially knew, all of whom were ready to dance the entire night away. She looked happy, she looked ready.

We started our set, Yacht pounding the drums alone at first. Within seconds, the mosh pit started—no elbows swung or roundhouse kicks or anything that threatened people's teeth, just folks pogoing in a circle and jumping in the air for flight and catching each other and smiling and smiling and smiling and singing when I start singing, even when they didn't know the words. Then there is Turtledove just as my black Telecaster and Duck's bass come roaring into the song. In a black Selena shirt, in the denim vest adorned with punk paraphernalia, with her bountiful black curly hair no longer confined to scrunchies and a hoodie's hood but wafting natural, loud, and free under the moonlight. She is in the circle; dancing, safe. I see her trip once, but Lucy and a Black femme pick her up, and she keeps running and jumping with everyone else.

No one stopped us. We didn't hear a single siren until the last of our feedback evaporated into the night air. Even then, Yacht shooed the cops away so the rest of us could keep dancing. Between sets, I talked to my people. All of them. Turtledove standing next to me throughout the night, fitting into my circles as though she'd been there for decades, as though this wasn't the second day we had ever seen each other. Sweat dried onto our clothes and skin—sweat from playing punk, sweat from dancing punk—but we hug, for the first time, refusing to let go of the backyard, our sweat synthesizing together. We witnessed the stars become stage lights for the punk that always made the most sense to us, we witnessed all the bodies alive in the dance circle, we witnessed everyone become a witness.

* * *

Here we are.

Punks, unbroken.

My left eye still aches from the bludgeoning left by BlueLives. Turtledove and I, however, are safe inside our home after curfew. We hear National Guardsmen march up and down our street, but we drown out their goosesteps with bathwater. Steam conceals me in the tub as my dreadlocks skate on the water. In the reflection, the good hair grows on the punks. Turtledove wraps naked arms around me, her breasts breathe the pulse of my torso. Our foreheads kiss. Lips on curls, lips on scars. Our fingers travel through the roots of each other's hair. Dirt, sweat, blood, all fall into the water and swim together in synchronized rhythms among the blues. We are clean soaking in one another's filth, floating tender in the water. We become feedback after a song's end: fading away, then echoing off the tile, soaring into beautiful noise.

Cacophonous.

Ours.

We fly.

Acknowledgments

For a minute, I really hated this book. Some of that ire came from how long this book lived with me before finding a home, then how much work needed to be done before being ready for publication. Some of it came from the fact that, even as I write this, I can't tell you what genre I wanted this book to be—fiction, nonfiction, poetry, all of them, none of them. Part of it, even, comes from knowing these writings existed in such different worlds, are contorted from a strange version of myself that I look back on and no longer recognize. I felt upset that I had to return to these distant worlds as often as I did, but then something clicked when finalizing what you are reading now: they are distant worlds, and that is worth celebrating. Maybe it's finally acknowledging growth as a person, maybe it's finally being at a place where I can confidently let these narratives live without wanting to change one or two things to make it "perfect" or whatever. Point is, I really hated this book for a minute. Now I don't. Now I love it again. Now I am ready for people to read it. Never thought I could get to this peace of mind, so I need to meditate on some folk who helped me get here—to this peace, to this love of this text.

As noted from the very start of this book, first and foremost, I want to thank Dr. Marlén Riós-Hernández for many things: being the first person to talk to me about punk rock in a discourse that made sense to our upbringings, being the inspiration to write a bunch of creative pieces about the tenderness and community of punk rock, being with me throughout the entirety of the writing process for this book as well as the PhD program, being with me throughout the Covid-19 lockdowns where I wrote the majority of these pieces (where, side note, we also discovered I love drag shows, she loves Animal Crossing, and we both love professional wrestling), for walking me through my many breakdowns and low moments as a writer, and for swiping right on Tinder and not ghosting me after I messaged first. All of it. Thank you, my punk rock angel.

I want to thank my parents, Reggie and Yadira, for not having a heart attack when I decided to go into writing and teaching rather than a "money-making profession," for being genuinely proud of my journey and still hanging my PhD acceptance letter on their refrigerator. Shout out, also, my immediate family: my sister, Bonnie; my nephew, Dylan; my uncle, Varito; and my grandma, Gladys. I apologize in advance that I will continue to write about our dark yet oh-so fascinating family histories.

Despite what some of the subtext and commentary might suggest, I am eternally grateful for the time I have and will continue to have playing with my band, tudors. David Moses Diaz and Christopher John Page are my musical brothers, my writing confidants, and they both hate having their middle names referred to in shout outs.

My community is anyone that left a mark on my life, people who either appeared explicitly or implicitly in these pages because their existence meant so much to my formation as a writer, an academic, a punk, a friend. I thank them all for allowing me into their lives: Erick Barrientos, Diego Valencia, Ahmad Munsaf, Rupal Patel, Kathy Avila, Cesar Lepe, Daniel Speer, James Goldmann, Nando Yiv, Chantal Lozano, Kathleen Rodriguez, Amira Ibrahim, Bryan Pinto, and Dennis Serrano (R.I.P.).

I thank my creative writing family, which is anyone who has suffered through a Master of Fine Arts or Doctorate of Philosophy writing program with me, who have seen and worked with either these specific pages, or pages that eventually bloomed into something

I became proud of, or sat with me in classrooms finding solace in a shared dread of academia while laughing and laughing and laughing into the void: AJ Urquidi, Casandra Hernandez-Rios, Taylor Mims, Zach Mann, Ramsey Matthews, Olivier Bochettas, Shane Eaves, Olivia Somes, Idalith Bustos, Janea Wilson, Toren Wallace, Kristen Skjonsby, Jax NTP, Chase Selby, Michael Benitez, Jen Aguilar, Kevin Parker, Jessica Drawbond, Cameron Lange, Melissa Chadburn, Tom Renjilian, Ben Bush, Jonathan Escoffery, Laura Roque, Erin Lynch, Alexandria Hall, Michelle Orsi, Lucas Lozada, Seth Fisher, Krishna Narayanamurti, Leesa Fenderson, Brian Lin, Tisha Reichle-Aguilera, and if you're reading this and read these pages in drafts prior and you're not here, please forgive me and feel free to find me and beat me up. Fun fact: David and Chris also belong in this category, but they already got their flowers a few paragraphs earlier. . . greedy bitches, I swear.

To writing professors, who have seen me grow, continue to ask about my journey, who have seen these pages, asked about these pages, critiqued these pages, who are currently seeking out new pages from me as we speak—Patty Seyburn, Bill Mohr, Maggie Nelson, David Treuer, Danzy Senna, Elda Maria Román, David St. John, Viet Thanh Nguyen, Dana Johnson, Jonathan Leal, Jackie Wang—I thank you all.

Writing programs themselves, however—with how they take advantage of hungry writers, underpay them, undermine their work, utilize white supremacist ideals to infantilize and invalidate marginalized people's truths, and leave many writers with very few resources heading into a hyper-competitive publishing landscape—can burn in hell.

Painfully early versions of a few of these pieces were given initial homes in the likes of *Passages North*, *Indiana Review*, *Apogee Journal*, *sin cesar* (formerly *Dryland*), *Joyland*, *The Oxford Handbook* of *Punk Rock*, and *Black Punk Now*. Special thanks to El Williams III for seeking me out personally, and a very special thanks to Chris L. Terry and James Spooner for keeping Black punk visibility alive and well in the music *and* writing worlds.

Of course, thank you Nightboat for taking a chance on *¡PÓNK!* back in October 2021. I didn't think the acceptance email was real for at least twenty-four hours, and I again apologize for looking like a deer in headlights during that first virtual meeting with Lindsey Boldt, Stephen Motika, Trisha Low, and Jaye Elizabeth Elijah. But y'all were so nice and inviting that it made publishing with Nightboat such an easy decision. Special shout to Jaye for reading this book 14,000,000 times to offer all the hardest yet necessary editorial suggestions to make this book its most authentic self. Through the fear, the changes, the grumpiness, the life-getting-in-all-our-ways, we got to the end with a much stronger book than I could have imagined. Also, thank you to Kazim Ali for taking that selfie with me at Pomona College when I mentioned I was being published by his press.

Though a healthy portion of this book is driven by autofictional and poetic narratives, every page is infused with nonfictional elements that I feel I must address, acknowledge, give flowers to, and highlight. So, I wish to acknowledge the following texts, videos, and speeches that informed or were cited in this manuscript:

- Audre Lorde, "The Master's Tools Will Never Dismantle the Master's House." *Sister Outsider: Essays and Speeches.*
- Malcom X interview at University of California, Berkeley, October 1963 with Professor John Legget and Herman Blake.
- *The Decline of Western Civilization*, 1981, directed by Penelope Spheeris.

- Lyrics used from the songs "Accrued Vacation Days (Daniel Listens to Krautrock Once)" and "To Us" by now defunct Long Beach post-hardcore band, Struckout.
- Gloria Anzaldúa, "How to Tame a Wild Tongue." *Borderlands: The New Mestiza - La Frontera.*
- Ariana Brown, "Dear White Girls in My Spanish Class."
- Frantz Fanon, "On Violence." *The Wretched of the Earth.*
- Dr. Alan Peláez Lopez, "The X In Latinx Is A Wound, Not A Trend."
- Ayishat Akanbi, Double Down News interview, November 2020.

For a book primarily propelled by music, it would feel wrong of me to not offer you this playlist comprised of songs that influenced or were directly referenced in *¡PÓNK!*:

- "Board Up" – Fuck U Pay Us
- "Racist, Sexist Boy" – The Linda Lindas
- "Politicians in My Eyes" – Death
- "Demolición" – Los Saicos
- "These Boots Are Made for Walking" – Pure Hell
- "We Don't Need the English" – The Bags
- "Inner City Blues (Make Me Wanna Holler)" – Marvin Gaye
- "While My Guitar Gently Weeps" – Specifically the live version with Tom Petty, Jeff Lynne, Steve Winwood, Dhani Harrison, and Prince.
- "Tourette's" – Nirvana
- "Volver, Volver" – Vicente Fernández
- "Holiday in Cambodia" – Dead Kennedys
- "Shit Brown" – tudors

- "Didn't It Rain" – Sister Rosetta Tharpe
- "Cold War" – Janelle Monáe
- "NegaNigger" – tudors
- "Walk Like a Panther" – Algiers
- "Accrued Vacation Days (Daniel Listens to Krautrock Once)" – Struckout
- "To Us" – Struckout
- "Por Tu Maldito Amor" – Vicente Fernández
- "Dos Gardenias" – Maria Rita
- "Purple Rain" – Prince
- "Boxcar" – Jawbreaker
- "Polite Young Man" – tudors

At the time of writing, I have no idea when this book will be released, so whoever you are, wherever you are, and *whenever* you are, thank you for reading it. Sincerely. 'Ppreciate chu.

MARCUS CLAYTON is a multi-genre Afrolatino writer from South Gate, CA, with an M.F.A. in Poetry from CSU Long Beach. Currently, he pursues a PhD in Literature and Creative Writing at the University of Southern California, focusing on the intersections between Latinx literature, Black literature, Decolonization, and Punk Rock. He has a poetry chapbook, *Nurture the Open Wounds*, with *Glass Poetry Press* and a few other publications included in *Indiana Review, Apogee Journal, Joyland Magazine, Passages North, Black Punk Now!*, and *The Oxford Handbook of Punk Rock*. *¡PÓNK!* is his first full-length book.

NIGHTBOAT BOOKS

Nightboat Books, a nonprofit organization, seeks to develop audiences for writers whose work resists convention and transcends boundaries. We publish books rich with poignancy, intelligence, and risk. Please visit nightboat.org to learn about our titles and how you can support our future publications.

The following individuals have supported the publication of this book. We thank them for their generosity and commitment to the mission of Nightboat Books:

Kazim Ali, Anonymous (5), Ava Avnisan, Jean C. Ballantyne, Bill Bruns, V. Shannon Clyne, The Estate of Ulla Dydo, Photios Giovanis, Amanda Greenberger, David Groff, Parag Rajendra Khandhar, Vandana Khanna, Shari Leinwand, Johanna Li, Elizabeth Madans, Martha Melvoin, Care Motika, Elizabeth Motika, The Leslie Scalapino – O Books Fund, Amy Scholder, Thomas Shardlow, Ira Silverberg, Benjamin Taylor, Jerrie Whitfield and Richard Motika, and Issam Zineh

This book is made possible, in part, by grants from the New York City Department of Cultural Affairs in partnership with the City Council, the New York State Council on the Arts Literature Program, and the Topanga Fund, which is dedicated to promoting the arts and literature of California.